DEAD GUILTY

A totally addictive crime thriller with a huge twist

(DI Calladine & DS Bayliss Book 9)

Helen H. Durrant

JOFFE BOOKS

First published 2019
Joffe Books, London
www.joffebooks.com

Please join our mailing list for free kindle crime thriller, detective, mystery, and romance books and new releases.
http://www.joffebooks.com/contact/

ISBN: 978-1-78931-105-1

Dedicated to Jasper, my brilliant publisher, for all his encouragement and efforts over the last few years.

PROLOGUE

They were as guilty as sin, and one way or another, he'd get even.

But in order to work out the detail, Bill Geddes needed peace and quiet to think. That was the difficult bit, what with the constant stream of well-wishers. For the umpteenth time that morning a stranger was at his side.

"Sorry, mate, I really am. You might not know me — I'm John Wells from the end of the street. Would have said something before, but I only heard this morning."

A clap on the shoulder, a gesture of sympathy. *Save it*, Geddes was tempted to reply. But he said nothing.

"You must have gone through hell these last days. I can't imagine how it feels."

He was right there. No one could. "I'd prefer if we didn't talk about it. The rawness still claws at my guts. Best if I just get on with things as usual."

A tight smile. The man appeared to understand. "When is the, you know, the . . . ?"

"The funeral?" No sense wrapping it up, that's what it was. "They tell me it can be as soon as the end of the week."

"Is that what you want?"

"No. I'm pushing for another post-mortem. They've missed something, I know it. My boy was murdered. I've told them, but no one will listen."

He saw doubt cloud the sympathiser's face. Why did everyone find it so hard to believe?

"That's quite an accusation, mate."

"He was murdered. Those bastards knew exactly what they were doing."

"Surely if that was true the police would have done more?"

Geddes laughed derisively. "They're useless! They haven't even looked for the culprits."

"Surely you told them about the . . . you know?"

"They're not interested. No real proof."

"Shame, but what can you do? Best thing is to put it all behind you. Lay your lad to rest and get on with your life."

"He deserves justice," Geddes replied angrily. "And I intend to make sure he gets it."

Wells made it sound simple. But it wasn't. The funeral wasn't the end of it. For everyone else the grieving would stop and things would go back to normal. But not for him. Normal was an indulgence, and he wouldn't waste time on grief either. Instead he would nurture the hate. In the end, it was *that* that would get him through.

Wells came a little closer. Geddes noticed that the man had a limp. "Some of us have been talking. You're right, the police are bloody useless. It's time we looked after ourselves. Give the bastards a taste of what they're short of. We meet in the Pheasant pub on the Hobfield a couple of times a week. Just give me a shout if you want in."

A nod goodbye, and he was gone. That was something else, people didn't hang about. They found conversation with him difficult. Geddes understood that. He didn't give a toss anyway. Let folk think what they wanted. They had no idea. No one had.

CHAPTER 1

Two weeks later

Tom Calladine's eyes snapped open.

A loud bang from downstairs had woken him. A quick glance at the bedside clock told him it was three thirty in the morning. What on earth! Getting out of bed, he pulled a bathrobe around his thickening frame and staggered onto the landing. He groaned, his bones felt stiff and his back ached. Layla, his paramedic girlfriend who lived across the road, had dragged him and the dog onto the moors above Leesdon yesterday. All this healthy living stuff was killing him. Despite what Layla would have him believe, he was too old for hill walking.

Listening in the dark, Calladine could hear footsteps downstairs. Someone was in the house. He'd lived in this small terraced house for donkey's years and never had any bother. But things were changing. Layla was constantly showing him posts on social media about local crimes, as if he needed telling! He'd read the statistics, he knew the score. It made her nervous so Sam, his dog, was staying at hers for the time being. Calladine felt suddenly outraged. This wasn't on. How dare someone break into his home! Time to confront the villain.

"What the hell are you doing?" he shouted, creeping up behind the little scroat, who was rifling through his bureau. He grabbed the lad by the hood, snatching it from his head. "I know you. You're Kat Barber's boy." Calladine had seen the lad working with a local builder. Now he was robbing houses. "Labouring not lucrative enough for you?"

"Let go!" Barber squirmed and hit Calladine with a metal object.

Calladine yelped in pain. As if his body didn't hurt enough! He grabbed the boy by the scruff of the neck and threw him to the ground. The weapon, a metal torch, spun out of reach.

Barber lay on his back. "Stay still," Calladine ordered, and pressed his foot on the lad's chest. "I take it you've got a phone?"

"Yeah."

"Ring your mother. Now!"

"Why would I do that, loser?"

The cheek of it! "If you don't, then I'll arrest you. You don't recognise me, do you? I'm a policeman, you idiot! Detective Inspector Calladine."

The lad's face was a picture, a mix of shock and disbelief. "Street reckoned an old git lived 'ere. I was told you'd be a pushover. I was told nowt about a bloody copper."

"Then Street's an idiot too, isn't he?"

"She won't be happy, my mam."

"That makes two of us. Now ring her. Tell her to get round here. She can deal with you."

Reluctantly, the lad made the call. It was the middle of the night so it took a few minutes before she answered. Kat Barber was angry. She was shouting so loudly that Calladine could hear her.

The lad ended the call. "She's on her way."

"This Street, what's his real name?" Calladine asked.

"Telling you nowt, copper. I'm no grass."

"What you are is a stupid kid who'll end up inside if he's not careful."

"Bugger off!" Then he asked, "Can I get up?"

Calladine pressed his foot down harder onto the lad's chest. "No. You can stay put. Dodging the question doesn't mean I won't keep asking, and eventually I will find out."

"No you won't, 'cos no one will talk. He's real mean, a hard man, is Street. No one's going to risk a beating."

Kat lived on the street that ran behind Calladine's. It only took a few minutes before she was banging on the front door.

"You can get up now," he told the lad.

His mother was in her nightgown and slippers. "What's our Sean done now?" She stormed in and cuffed her son across the side of his head. "Do you know what time it is? What the hell are you playing at?"

"He broke in," Calladine said. "I caught him searching through my stuff. Not that there's much here. No jewellery or money to speak of."

Sean glanced around the room. "That laptop over there would have done."

Calladine glared at him. "Reckons he's working with a villain called Street. Did you know that?"

Kat took another swipe at the boy. This time the flat of her hand connected with his cheek. Calladine winced, she packed a hefty punch.

"How many times do I have to tell you? Get involved with that villain and you'll end up inside." She turned to Calladine. "I'm sick of telling him, but does he listen? Does he hell. This Street is a bad 'un, into all sorts. Got all the local lads, including this dollop, wrapped round his little finger. What with him and these vigilantes that're wandering the streets at night, it's bloody warfare out there. This one's terrified of meeting them down an alley one dark night."

"Doesn't keep him at home though, does it?" Scared or not, Sean Barber was still robbing houses. But the idea of vigilantes was new to Calladine. "Street? Is that all you've got?"

Sean nodded. "No one knows his real name. But them vigilantes are real enough and deadly serious. Gave Wilco a beating the other night just because he was hanging about outside the late shop. Accused him of staking out the place."

"And was he?"

Sean shrugged.

"How did you get in here?" Calladine asked him.

"Kitchen window. Broke it and forced the lock, sorry."

That must have been the bang that woke him, Calladine realised.

"What're you going do with him, Mr Calladine?" Kat asked. "Is it a night in the nick? To be honest, I could do with the rest."

Calladine could see that she wasn't joking. Her face was pale, the skin around her eyes dark and heavy. The lad himself had his head down, hands in his hoodie pockets. Calladine doubted he was really sorry, but dragging the pair of them down to the station would serve no purpose.

Calladine shook his head. "No, you take him home and deal with him. He can pay for the damage."

"What with, got nowt," came the sullen reply.

Calladine took hold of the lad by the front of his hoodie. "You'll pay for that window by the weekend or you *will* go inside. Do I make myself clear?"

"I'll make sure he does." Kat grabbed her son's arm. "Say thank you to Mr Calladine. He's given you another chance. Not that you deserve it."

The lad grunted something.

"I'll send him round with the money, don't you worry," she said.

Calladine opened the front door for them.

"I've been in this house before, with my mum," Kat said, glancing around. "She and your mum were good friends. They used to go to the 'knit and natter' group at the community centre together. Whenever I was off school my mum would take me along with her."

Calladine smiled, he wasn't surprised. His late mum, Freda Calladine, had been well known in the town. He turned to Sean. "This is your last chance, laddie," Calladine warned. "Come within my sights again and I won't be so soft. You're only getting off this time because your mother's a neighbour."

CHAPTER 2

Day 1

Calladine arrived at Leesdon station just after seven a.m. He was the first one in. After the incident with Sean Barber in the night he hadn't been able to sleep. This young villain, Street, had taken control of the younger element in the area, got them robbing houses and all riled up about vigilantes. Calladine didn't like it. Task for the day — find out what was going on and who this 'Street' person was.

Calladine got straight to work searching for Street on the police computer system. When he found nothing, he resorted to social media. He was so deeply engrossed that he didn't notice DCI Rhona Birch enter the office and sit her bulky frame down opposite him.

She coughed. "We have a problem, Inspector," she began. "DI Long has had a heart attack."

Birch was not one for going around the houses. Calladine looked up from the screen. It took a moment or two for the words to sink in. Brad Long was younger than him, and had seemed fine last week. Mind you, he was a few stone heavier, drank a lot, and was fond of his 'full English' breakfasts. Or heart attack on a plate, as Layla called them.

"He collapsed yesterday while out on an investigation. Paramedics took him to Wythenshawe. He's had a stent fitted. According to his wife, he should make a decent recovery."

"That's something at least. Will he return to work, ma'am?"

"I imagine so, but he'll be on light duties for a while. No stress. You know the kind of thing."

No stress? That was a big ask in a job like this. "A warning to us all, I suppose." Calladine's sober reply. "What about his workload? Is DS Thorpe able to cope?"

"No, not without guidance. Sergeant Thorpe flounders under pressure. Long was working on a new case, a big one." She sighed. "Yesterday afternoon we received a call about a child abduction — Sophie Alder. Long was investigating. We can't delay, you will have to take over."

Calladine frowned. This was serious. "Abduction, ma'am? How old is the child?"

"Three. She is the daughter of Richard Alder. A well-known name about these parts, I believe. He has money and influence, and wants action fast. Not that that will have any bearing on how seriously we deal with this. Of course, a missing child always merits all our best efforts." She heaved another sigh. "Plus, he knows the new chief super. Apparently, they are members of the same country club. If we don't get on top of this fast, we'll have Isaac Chesworth breathing down our necks."

They certainly didn't want that. Detective Chief Superintendent Chesworth had inherited the job after Angus Ford had been arrested for murder, and currently had responsibility for both Leesworth and Oldston stations.

"Chesworth aside, I'm sure any parent would be distraught," Calladine reminded her.

Birch nodded. "Alder has been on the phone already this morning. He's frantic with worry. I want to give him something positive, but as yet, we have nothing. Long's theory is that whoever took the child will demand money for her safe return. Given the family's wealth, that could well be the

case. Pull out all the stops. I want headway on this urgently."
The DCI stood up and left Calladine with his thoughts.

Alder was indeed well known, although Calladine had never met him. As a boy, Richard Alder had lived on the Hobfield, a notorious housing estate in Leesdon. The place had spawned so many villains, Calladine had lost count. But Alder was an anomaly. He'd never been in trouble, and in recent years had made good. He'd got himself a fistful of qualifications from college, and eventually started his own business. Today he employed more people in the Leesworth area than anyone else, even Buckley Pharmaceuticals, owned by Calladine's birth mother, Eve Buckley. He had a factory on the industrial estate, manufacturing cakes and biscuits. His products were on supermarket shelves across the country. He was generous, too. Gave large donations to local charities. Birch might be right. Alder had money, and that might well be the reason behind the kidnap.

"Have you heard about Long?" Ruth Bayliss asked. She'd just arrived. Ruth was his sergeant and long-time friend. Dumping her bag in her desk drawer, she smoothed down her skirt and sat down. "Can't say I'm surprised. He's a lazy sod, barely moves off his arse if he can help it."

Calladine couldn't help smile. She was right. "How did you find out? Birch has only just told me."

"Jungle drums. Thorpe told Rocco and he rang me last night."

"No one rang me," Calladine retorted, miffed at being left out.

"Sorry, Tom, I was up to my eyes in it. We're decorating. Tearing paper off walls is hard work."

Calladine was pleased. Decorating meant that all was well again between Ruth and Jake. They'd been going through a tough time recently. If they split up, he knew Ruth would put on a brave face, but in reality, she'd be devastated. The couple were good together and, of course, they had their toddler son Harry. "A heart attack though, Ruth. That's serious."

"You should be grateful to Layla for keeping you on your toes. Without her, you'd be a Mr Blobby and at risk yourself. Mind you, you've slacked a bit recently."

Calladine frowned. "My waistline's just fine, thank you." He glanced down at his middle. She was right, he had put some weight on. "It's alright for you. You're naturally slim. And I'm a good few years older. It's hard, put it on and it won't shift."

"Rubbish! It's just a matter of discipline, and it takes work," she corrected him. "I watch what I eat and I go to the gym. You could come with me. It's only down the road from your house."

He ran a hand through his close cropped, greying hair. It might suit Ruth, but there was no way he could do the gym thing. "I'll make my own arrangements if it's all the same."

She got up from her desk and made for the coffee machine. "Want one?"

Calladine shook his head. Whatever regime Ruth followed it was working. She was a lot slimmer than she'd once been. Her hair was longer, too. A warm shade of chestnut and resting on her shoulders. He didn't take much notice as a rule, but lately Ruth was looking quite the stunner.

"What're you doing in so early anyway?" she asked him, returning to her desk with a steaming mug.

"I couldn't sleep. My house was broken into last night."

Ruth's eyebrows shot up. "You're joking! They've got some nerve. It's coming to something when the little sods break into a copper's house."

"And I know his mother. Stupid kid's a neighbour." He logged off the system and sat back in his chair.

"Did you tackle him?"

"Damn right I did."

Ruth shook her head at him. "Risky that, Tom. He could have left you for dead."

Ignoring the comment, he asked, "Have you heard of an individual called Street?"

Ruth frowned. "I don't think so. But I'll keep an ear out. Why?"

"Just something the kid said. Did you know that Leesdon has a bunch of vigilantes wandering the streets?"

"I did see something on a poster in the local shop. I don't think it's anything serious, Tom. A few locals had a meeting about vandalism, theft and the like. Decided to post anything they discovered in a Facebook group. It's about keeping an eye on things, warning each other to be mindful, that's all."

Calladine would reserve judgement until he knew more. He took the bundle of paperwork handed to him by a uniformed officer and flicked through the pages, his eyes scanning the detail. "We've inherited the missing Sophie Alder case off Brad. Long started the investigation but given the heart attack, Birch has passed it to us. Forensics have made a start. We need to speak to the parents, find out for ourselves what happened and then we'll go and see what Julian's turned up."

"Thorpe mentioned it yesterday morning before Long took ill. Child abduction." Ruth shivered. "It's been a while since we had one of those. The parents must be worried sick. I don't know the father, but I've met Annie, the little girl's mother. She used to bring Sophie to the same nursery as my Harry." Ruth paused, remembering. "She's a pretty little girl, big blue eyes and blonde hair."

"Have you seen their house?" Calladine asked.

"I've driven past, it's up near your mother, Eve's. A huge pile of stone and glass on the hill above Hopecross. I remember Annie boasting that Rick Alder had designed it himself. Must have cost a fortune."

"Got it to spend, hasn't he? Alder is very much the local lad made good. Nice bloke, d'you reckon?"

"I suppose he must be. Annie's okay, too. But underneath that delicate exterior she's a tough cookie. Brought up on the Hobfield, the pair of them. I doubt she'd stand any nonsense."

DC Simon Rockliffe, known as Rocco, and DC Alice Bolshaw arrived at the office together, deep in conversation about last night's televised football match. The two of them had been in a relationship for a few weeks, but were now just good friends.

"We've got the Alder case," Calladine announced to the team. "Get the background checks done on the family," he said, turning to Rocco. "See if you can work out who would want to take the child."

Rocco nodded.

"Want me to help him, sir?" Alice asked.

He shook his head. "No thanks, Alice. I want you to look at social media and then get out into the town and ask questions. See what you can find out about a lad who goes by the name of 'Street.' Anything and everything. Report back later."

CHAPTER 3

Ruth stared enviously at the hillside mansion in front of her. "Who'd have thought it of that pair. There was a time when they couldn't raise a couple of quid between them."

"House this size is a waste of money," Calladine responded, regarding the Alder family home. "The heating bill alone must be astronomical."

"Trust you, skinflint! Even so, not bad given how young he is and where he came from."

Calladine shrugged. "A little excessive though, given there is only the three of them. What's wrong with the simple life? That's what I say."

"He's made a fortune and likes to spend it. Nothing wrong with that, good for the local economy. The bill for the wedding alone must have run into thousands."

"D'you know what I'm thinking?" Calladine asked, staring at the property in front of him.

Ruth looked at him. "I can guess. The family live up here in semi-isolation, have plenty of money and are well known. Alder makes no secret of his wealth. In some respects, he rubs folk's faces in it. The *I came from one of the worst estates in the area and look at me now* syndrome."

"You're thinking along the same lines as me then? That Long's theory is correct. Someone thinks Alder needs teaching a lesson, reminding of his roots. Someone takes the child and demands money for her safe return."

"I hope you're right, Tom, but there are no guarantees."

"A body hasn't been found yet," Calladine reminded her.

Ruth suddenly felt cold. "What a dreadful thought. Poor little girl, wherever she is. We must tread carefully. If they've had a demand for money already, they won't want to talk to us."

"Does Alder have any enemies?"

"Can't say I know much about him," Ruth replied. "But he's in business. It'll be as cut-throat as any other, so I suppose he must have some enemies. But someone evil enough to take his child, well, that's something else."

"That is our priority. We need to know Alder's background in detail. The good stuff and the dirt. C'mon then, let's make a start."

Calladine left the car parked by the tall gates at the entrance and the two detectives walked up the wide shingle drive.

Calladine glanced around. "Odd atmosphere, don't you think?"

"That's a weird thing to say, especially coming from you," Ruth smiled. "But you're right. You're a local lad, don't you realise where this is?"

"Should I?"

"Alder bought the land, but before he could build, he had to knock down the ruins of the existing building. This is the site of the old workhouse, remember that?"

Calladine threw her look. "How bloody old d'you think I am?"

She laughed. "You might remember it. The place stood here until the late seventies, but thankfully it's been empty since the turn of the century. It had a dreadful history. Cruelty to kids, folk going missing — the things they got away with beggars belief."

"Why the interest?"

"An ancestor of mine was put in there. Nineteen, no husband, and pregnant. Fortunately, she got out and skipped off to America. But no one knows for sure what happened to the kid. Records show he was both born and died here. There is a family tale that she smothered him."

"Hadn't got you down as a family history buff."

"I've just started to do the research, Tom. It was speaking to Greco when he was with us that did it. He's really into this stuff."

"He's a weirdo, don't forget. I wouldn't be copying him." DCI Stephen Greco had helped them out with a recent case, but paid a fanatical attention to detail. It did not make him popular.

"You just don't like him. He's okay, gets a bit obsessive, but he's been a great help with the info I needed to get going with this."

"Don't encourage him, that's my advice," Calladine warned.

"I thought you two had made your peace?"

"We have, but things stand a better chance of staying peaceful if we give each other a wide berth."

Ruth grinned. "He's a bloody good detective. The pair of you have a lot in common."

This came as a surprise. "You think so! Nevertheless, he's not someone I'd want to have around every working day, put it that way."

They'd reached the front door and Ruth pressed the bell. A young woman answered. She was about twenty, with short dark hair. She was dressed in a cropped top and tight jeans, with frayed holes in the knees.

"They don't want to see anyone," she announced and made to close the door.

"They'll see us. We're police." Calladine showed her his warrant card.

"What about the one who came yesterday?"

"He's been taken ill. We've been assigned the case in his absence. Is the family in?"

"Annie is. In a state, as usual," she said. "There's always something with her. Nothing's ever simple."

Given what had happened, Calladine was surprised at her attitude. Was this girl totally without feeling?

"And you are?" Ruth asked.

"Frankie. Francesca Halliwell. Annie's sister."

"Were you here yesterday when Sophie went missing?" she asked.

"No. It was Joanne who raised the alarm. Annie rang me and made me come over. She might be the big sister, but where the kid's concerned, that one's never learned to cope. Always in a panic about something."

Ruth glanced at Calladine. She wanted to say something, blast the girl for making the kidnap of a child sound like nothing important. She bit her tongue.

Frankie Halliwell stood aside and gestured down the hallway. A pair of double doors led to a palatial sitting room where a willowy blonde with a tear-stained face sat on a plush velvet sofa. Another young woman was pacing the floor.

"Please tell me you've found her," Annie Alder sobbed, fear evident in her blue eyes. "This nightmare has to stop or I'll go out of my mind. My Sophie has never been away from home before. She'll be terrified."

"DI Calladine and DS Bayliss," he introduced them both. "We're doing everything we can, Mrs Alder," Calladine assured her. "We're here today to go over what happened. No detail is too small. We need to know everything."

"I got that about ten minutes ago. I was in the throes of ringing the station when you arrived." Annie nodded at a printed sheet on the coffee table in front of her. "There's not much, but it's confirmation that someone has taken my Sophie, and that she's okay for the time being."

"Was it pushed through the door?" Calladine asked, picking it up.

"No, email. I printed it out. The laptop is there — I suppose you'll want that."

Calladine nodded. "Do you have another one, in case the kidnapper makes further contact by email?"

Annie nodded. "There's a workstation in the office. I can log on to that."

Calladine read the note. *She's safe now*. The words were accompanied by a picture of a child playing with toys on a rug.

"This is your daughter?"

Annie nodded.

"Do you recognise where this photo was taken?"

"It's a red rug, what is there to recognise?" she said sharply.

"Are any of the toys in the photo Sophie's?"

"No. The kidnapper must have provided them. It had been wet. The kids didn't take anything of their own outside."

The wording of the note was odd. Not the usual stuff of ransom demands. No threat was made. And why did someone think that Sophie needed a place of safety?

"No family liaison here?" Calladine asked, glancing at Ruth.

"I sent them away," Annie replied angrily. I didn't want strangers hanging around, reporting back on our every word, our every move. Joanne is staying with me." She nodded at the woman with her. "She's a friend and looks after Sophie part-time when I'm working."

"Don't forget me," Frankie reminded her. "You ring, I jump. Isn't that how it works?"

"Family liaison will keep you updated, that's all," Calladine said. "They are here to help, not to spy." He sat down on a chair opposite her. "There's no news yet, I'm afraid," he told her gently. "Would you describe to us exactly what happened yesterday."

Annie swore under her breath. "How many times do I have to go over this? Don't you lot talk to each other?"

"Yes, we do, but my colleague has since become ill and is not able to tell me what he knows. Apart from which, I prefer to hear it from you."

Annie sighed. "Sophie was playing outside with another of Joanne's little charges, a lad called Jack. Joanne went to bring them in, but couldn't see Sophie anywhere. According to Jack, she'd been talking to a man by the back gate."

"Did this man know Sophie's name? Did your daughter recognise him?" Ruth asked.

"Jack said so," Joanne confirmed. "He told me that he called to her by her name."

"You didn't watch them, check on them periodically?" asked Ruth.

Joanne looked uncomfortable. "Annie was showing me the wedding photos," she said. "We were chatting. Time flew past."

"Besides, the garden is secure," Annie added. "We have high fencing, a thick privet hedge. And the wooden gate at the back is always locked."

"Well, someone opened that gate," Calladine reminded her. "The little lad said a man was standing there?" Joanne nodded. "Then he must have either broken the lock or had a key."

"The forensic people that came yesterday said it was broken," Joanne said.

"How often do you use the gate?" Calladine directed the question at Annie.

"Rarely, to be honest. We're so far out that when we leave this place I usually drive. The back gate leads out onto the side of the hill and then up into the woods."

"When exactly did you last see your daughter, Mrs Alder?" Ruth asked.

Annie started to weep. "I don't know. They were playing. I didn't take much notice of the time."

"They went outside at about three. Remember?" Joanne looked at Annie for confirmation. "It had stopped raining so we decided they could have a runabout in the garden."

"Do I have to stay?" Frankie Halliwell broke in. She was leaning against the wall, a bored expression on her face. "I'm supposed to be meeting some mates later."

"For God's sake, Frankie. Have some thought for your sister," Joanne snapped at her.

"Keep your hair on! The brat's safe — you can see that from the photo. It'll be someone's idea of a joke."

The outburst shocked Ruth in particular. Someone had taken Annie's child — it was every parent's nightmare.

"This is no joke," Ruth assured her, coolly. "It is a very serious matter."

Frankie shrugged. "Email says she's safe, or can't you read? I can't help, anyway. I know nowt."

"For goodness sake stop whining, Frankie. Do what you want. I'm past caring," Annie said.

"Don't expect me back tonight either. I've got better things to do than listen to you going on." Frankie stormed out.

"Do you have cameras outside?" Calladine asked.

"Only at the front of the house," Annie answered him. "We never got round to sorting out the back garden."

"Do you mind if I take a look?"

Annie Alder nodded.

Calladine left the women alone.

* * *

"Do you remember me, Annie?" Ruth asked gently once Calladine was out of the way. She sat facing Annie on the sofa. "I know you from the nursery in Leesdon. My little boy, Harry, goes there. He and Sophie were great pals at one time."

Annie gave a half-hearted smile. "It's Ruth, isn't it? I recognised you at once. Sorry I didn't say anything. I'm a mess, and Frankie doesn't help. I shouldn't have rung her. This is a nightmare. I can't believe what's happening." She picked up the printed sheet and shook it angrily. "What is this about? What does he want from me?"

"If you take the email at face value — then nothing. But it may be followed quite soon with a demand for money," Ruth told her. "Has there been any further contact?"

The room fell silent. Annie shook her head. "No. No one has contacted me. But I can't speak for Rick."

"The email isn't signed. Do you have any idea who might want to do this? Anyone given you a hard time recently?"

"Not that I can think of. But where Rick is concerned, who can say? He gets off on rubbing folk up the wrong way." She let out a sob. "I thought we had it all. That he loved us. How wrong could I have been? These days he prefers the company of his new friend, Giles Pennington, to us. Pennington only has to snap his fingers and Rick jumps."

"Has anyone been critical of how Sophie was being brought up? Perhaps a relative or a friend?"

"What are you saying? That I'm a crap mother, is that it?"

Ruth tapped the printed sheet of paper. "No, not at all Annie. I see the words on this email, 'She's safe now,' and I have to ask. They suggest to me that perhaps someone thinks that has not always been the case."

Annie was sobbing again. This was getting them nowhere. "Where is your husband?" Ruth asked.

That particular question opened the floodgates. "Not here, is the short answer. Our daughter has been kidnapped and Rick has a meeting to go to," she wailed. "He doesn't give a damn, and that's the truth."

Ruth handed her a tissue from a box on the coffee table. "I'm sure that can't be true. DI Calladine told me that he's already phoned the station this morning. He has a business to run. People rely on him."

Annie glowered at Ruth. "There are times when I hate him!"

The venom was real and it shocked Ruth. Like most local folk, she knew the story. Annie and Rick had been together since their early teens. Their recent wedding had been long anticipated and had enjoyed a centre spread in the local press.

"Come on, Annie, you don't mean that." Joanne took hold of her friend's hand. "You remember what it was like being brought up on the Hobfield? The grinding poverty, the 'making do.' We both said we'd get out if it was the last thing we did." Joanne grinned. "Well, you did it with bells on, kid. You're wed to the richest man in town. Live in the biggest house in the area. And made every woman for miles around jealous as hell."

Annie glared at her friend. "You think that's all I care about? Rick's money? I don't care about any of that. I just want Sophie back. Rick's selfish. His business has always come first. I swear he only stays with me because of Sophie."

"It's the shock talking," Ruth said. "I'm sure Rick will return just as soon as he's able."

"Perhaps." Annie did not sound convinced. "Do you know what I think?" She had a defiant look on her face. "I think the wedding was merely a ploy to keep the peace. Up until a couple of months ago, Rick wasn't keen. He thought we were fine as we were. But I kept going on. I wanted proper security for Sophie. In the end, he gave in. But I think the whole event was his way of keeping me occupied and out of his hair." Annie Alder looked Ruth in the eye. They were cold, hard, and Ruth shuddered inwardly. "Find my little girl. I can't stay with Rick without her."

CHAPTER 4

"Get anything?" Calladine asked Ruth as they walked back to the car.

"The laptop." She had it tucked under her arm. "And a recent photo of Sophie Alder. We'll need one if there's to be an appeal."

"Any gossip? Any hint that all is not as it seems? There was a right atmosphere in there."

Ruth's expression hardened. "That was down to the sister, Frankie. First-class attention seeker that one."

"Anything else?"

"Annie more than hinted that she and Alder are not the loving couple everyone imagines them to be. All she wants is the child back. Without her, their relationship has no meaning."

"Not quite the stuff of fairy tales then. Does Annie suspect her husband of taking the child?"

"No, she's just upset. It's his lack of input Annie is livid about, and I can't blame her. Just when she needs him, Alder goes missing, and that sister of hers is something else! Nasty piece of work, she is. Where Alder is concerned, the business comes first, even before the threat to their daughter. I find that very odd. You'd think his PA would be able to keep things ticking over at work. Even though they've been married for such a short time, Annie's had enough. She's woken up to the reality of what life with Alder will be like."

Calladine pursed his lips. "You saw the email. 'She's safe now.' Do you think the girl has been kidnapped or taken by someone concerned for the child's welfare?"

Ruth frowned. "It's a difficult one. There has been no ransom demand yet. Whoever has the child may be playing a game, letting the pressure build. That will drive Annie nuts. I know it would if it were me."

Calladine paused. "The lock on the gate was forced. It looks as if it was jemmied off. But apart from that it is a secure garden."

"Someone breaks the lock on the back gate and no one hears or sees anything? Surely the thing would blow open in the wind."

"We'll speak to Julian, see what he has to say. While I was wandering around, I bumped into the gardener. He knew nothing about the gate either. Comes once a month, that's all. But they do have other staff. We will have to interview them all."

"Whoever took the child must have planned it," Ruth put to him. "They knew she was here, knew about the gate, and worked out what needed doing to get to her. This wasn't an opportunist attempt, Tom."

Calladine nodded in agreement. "I think you're right. I also think the child knew whoever took her. You're a mum, what would the normal reaction be? Would your Harry run to anyone who called him?"

Ruth shook her head firmly. "No. I tell him constantly about talking to strangers. And you're right. We will have to talk to the little boy, Jack, see what his take on it was."

"Despite what Annie Alder says, I want family liaison with her. Should contact be made, we need to know about it fast."

* * *

It took the pair half an hour to reach the Duggan Centre, the forensic facility they used. The senior forensic scientist in charge was Professor Julian Batho, a valued expert, and a friend of theirs.

Julian was not given to humour, and lately he hadn't smiled much. He had been engaged to another member of Calladine's team, DC Imogen Goode, until her murder during a case. Julian was still struggling with the loss.

Calladine gave the scientist a cheery smile. "Okay, Julian?" He lived in hope that Julian might be starting to recover from his grief. "We've inherited the Alder child abduction case off Long," Calladine said. "CSI were there yesterday. Did you turn up anything?"

"The gate in the garden," Julian began. "The lock had been broken some time ago and the thing had been wired together so that it would not swing open inadvertently." He held up a clear plastic bag containing some twisted wire. "Apparently, the gate is rarely used, so it wasn't noticed. For whoever took the child, it was a simple matter of a few twists and they were in. There were splinters of wood lying on the ground. The grass had grown over some of them, so I'd say the lock had been dealt with sometime in the past."

Calladine frowned. "Planned then. We thought as much."

"We'll run tests on the wire but I wouldn't get your hopes up. The wood splinters, however, are another matter. We collected them and found a substance on some. If it proves to be blood, we might get a DNA match."

"Whoever bust the lock hurt himself in the process. Nice one." Calladine smiled. "Let me know as soon as you have the results. Annie Alder got an email this morning." He handed over her laptop.

Julian nodded. "I'll pass it to the tech people."

"We'll likely be in the Wheatsheaf Friday teatime if you want to join us?" Ruth offered. "A couple of pints with the gang, catch up on the gossip. What d'you say? Do you good to get out."

Julian looked at her with his hangdog expression. "I'll see," he said at last. "I might be busy."

She patted his arm. It was no good pushing him. "You know where we are if you fancy it."

Ruth joined Calladine in the corridor. "He's hard work."

"He could do with finding another woman. It's been a while since Imogen. A dose of romance might fix him," Calladine said.

Ruth grinned. "Like it fixed you, you mean?"

Before he could reply, a female voice called out. "Tom, Ruth, what are you pair doing here? Not more work is it?"

It was Natasha Barrington, one of the Home Office pathologists who worked at the Duggan. She'd helped the team with a number of recent cases.

Calladine smiled at her. "No, you can relax, Natasha. We're here to see Julian. Why, got a lot on?"

"We always do," she said. "I'll walk with you to the car park."

"Out for lunch?" Ruth asked as they left the building.

The pathologist looked solemn. "No. I'm going to speak to a grieving parent, try to convince him that a second PM on his son is not the answer. Not an easy one."

"Not your usual role," Calladine said.

"He's spoken to everyone else. I'm the last resort. Remember that concert up on Clough Hill this summer?"

Calladine nodded. "Rowdy, got out of hand. Had to get officers in from Oldston to help sort the rabble. Not that I attended."

"As is usual, there were a number of casualties. But there was also one tragic death. The victim was young, a twenty-year-old local lad. You may know him — Alex Geddes, the son of a man called Bill Geddes."

Calladine shook his head. The names meant nothing to him.

"According to those who saw him, Alex was drinking solid for the entire day and he took a number of pills. You might recall there was a batch of dodgy ecstasy doing the rounds. Alex became ill and was admitted to Leesdon Infirmary. Sadly, they couldn't do much for him. Despite the excessive amount of alcohol in his system, the death was attributed to a bad reaction to the pills. The usual hospital post-mortem was conducted."

"And the parents can't accept it?" Calladine asked.

"There's only the father, and he's having none of it. He believes his son was got at in some way. Had the booze and pills foisted on him, and didn't know any better than to take them."

"Twenty years old?" Ruth looked sceptical. "He must have known what he was doing."

"You'd think so. But Geddes has asked for a second PM, and is refusing to organise the funeral until he gets one. I've got a copy of the report from the original PM to show him and just hope it makes him see sense."

"He's lost his son and doesn't know what to do. It's understandable in a way," Ruth said. "But he can't refute the PM. If there was anything, it would have been found, surely?"

Natasha frowned. "I've known them miss things. Hospital post-mortems for deaths that have a known cause, or are not suspicious, are different from the ones we carry out at the Duggan, less rigorous, shall we say. The pathologist at the hospital can do up to five at a time. They don't even use different scalpels."

A shudder went down Ruth's spine. "You've got your work cut out," she said. "I don't envy you."

CHAPTER 5

"I've got as much background as I can find on Alder," Rocco reported when Calladine and Ruth arrived back at the station. "It's as expected — pillar of the community, climbed high very fast and appears to be reaping the rewards."

"What d'you mean, appears? Is he doing well or not?" Calladine asked.

"It's the figures, sir. Granted the factory is profitable. He's expanded fast, there are new buildings and equipment. I checked the statistics on Companies House website. There are no financial problems that I can see. The only thing I'd question is where the money came from for both that expansion and the house he had built. It wasn't in the profits he's made over the past few years. Despite the business being solvent, given the spending, there's quite a shortfall. A look at his bank accounts would be interesting."

"Alder isn't a suspect, he's the victim," Calladine reminded Rocco. "We'd never get a warrant."

"He could have got a loan?" Ruth suggested.

"The amounts are huge," Rocco told them. "The bank or whoever must be backing him up to the hilt."

"He's a safe bet," Calladine shrugged. "Alder's business is now the biggest employer in this area."

"Even bigger than Buckley's?" Ruth queried.

"Yes, I should say so. The rapid expansion has seen to that. Anything else?"

"He's recently married his childhood sweetheart, Annie."

"All is not as it appears there," Ruth told them. "So double-check. Look for dirt — I'm sure there must be some. Sweetheart or not, Annie expressed doubt about their relationship when we saw her this morning. Odd, don't you think, for a pair of newlyweds? And while you're at it, have a look at Frankie Halliwell, Annie's younger sister. She struck me as trouble. Check if she's on the system."

Calladine flicked through his emails. There was the expected report from Julian outlining what he'd already told them. The blood found on the wood splinters was crucial. That and the fact they were sure that the child, Sophie, had known her abductor. That meant it had to be a family friend or relative.

"Ruth, you know Annie, go and see her again. You are a familiar face, she might open up to you. See if you can get anything else out of her. And check if the family are known to social services."

"I wouldn't have thought they'd have attracted their attention," Ruth said.

"You're forgetting where they came from. Richard Alder still has family on the Hobfield. A father and an older brother. I presume the family see them?"

"I would imagine Alder rarely sets foot on the estate these days."

"Nonetheless, they are still his family. Find out if Alder has ever been pressured to help them financially. Perhaps he refused and they've taken matters into their own hands. You might see if either his father, Alf, or his brother, Billy, is on our system too."

"You think Sophie's grandfather took her?" Ruth looked dubious. "Alf Alder is a drunk, he's in the pub most nights. He isn't the childminding type."

"What about the brother? Billy?"

"Don't know much about him."

"Find out. Get the details up there," he nodded at the incident board.

"Inspector Calladine!"

It was DCI Birch.

"My office. I'd like an update on the Alder case."

Calladine dutifully followed her into her office. "Not much to tell yet, ma'am. We're chasing forensics and there has been communication from whoever took the child. Not asking for money though, simply stating that she's safe."

"Safe for now," she said. "I've had Richard Alder on the phone again. He is not a happy man. He wants action and quick. Doesn't think we're throwing our all into this."

"The team are on it, ma'am. From what we've been told, we believe the child knew the person who took her."

"I've had Chesworth on too. He's asking for updates on a daily basis. I do not want him here," she insisted. "This must be sorted urgently. I suggest you take Thorpe under your wing and make optimum use of uniform to help with the legwork. They'll complain. Apparently, there's a run of petty crime locally."

"Yes, I know," he responded. "My home was broken into last night."

"Did you report it?"

"No, ma'am. I know him, he's a neighbour. Got his mother to deal with him. Far more effective," he smiled.

Birch frowned. "We shouldn't give them an inch. These young villains see it as weakness."

"Not much we can do though, is there, ma'am. We don't have the manpower to walk the streets. They have a new leader, too. Not a name I've heard before, but whoever this 'Street' is, he's got some clout."

Birch's face clouded. "What did you say? Street?"

"Yes, ma'am. He's the new villain encouraging the recent mayhem. I've been trying to find out who he is, but there's nothing."

"Drop it."

Calladine paused. "With respect, ma'am, I can't. He's behind most of the robberies. It's vital that I find him for questioning."

"Leave this, Calladine. I won't tell you again." Birch's eyes were hard.

"Can I ask why, ma'am?"

"No, you can't. We'll discuss this another time." She paused. "I'm not oblivious to what's going on, you know. I do look at the crime statistics for the area. But that's not our prime concern right now. Our priority has to be the Alder girl."

"We'll do our best, ma'am," he said.

"I want her found. Alder has a lot of influence. We do not want to make an enemy of him."

"We could get the press involved, ask the parents to make an appeal?" Calladine suggested.

"I've already put that to him, but he's not keen."

Calladine was surprised. "Why not? If whoever took her is known to the family, the glare of publicity could have them running scared."

"I explained how it would work, but he's having none of it. As far as Alder is concerned, the fewer people who know, the better."

Calladine couldn't work out why Alder would shy away like this. Back in the incident room he made a note on the board.

"Annie has been given a sedative and is resting," Ruth said. "Frankie, the sister, doesn't think she'll be awake before the morning."

"Okay, try again then." He sat down at his desk. "This is a weird one. I know the kid is missing but something is wrong. The email with no ransom demand. The fact that the boy, Jack, reckons it was someone Sophie knew."

"An inside job?" Ruth asked. "But why? I can't see any reason, can you?"

"We're missing something, Ruth. But what exactly?"

CHAPTER 6

The fist hit the lad full in the face, sending him reeling backwards, cracking his head against the wall.

"You hold him tight and I'll empty his pockets," Bill Geddes told one of the men. Like the others, Geddes had a scarf over the lower half of his face, and a hood over his head. After his chat with John Wells, he'd decided to take him up on the offer, and meet the group. He needed an outlet for the rage. Beating up the thieving ruffians who were terrorising his town would do for now.

"Well, look at this," he said, holding up a bag of small wraps. "The little git's a user." He lashed out again, sending the lad flying to the floor. "Who did you get this off?" Geddes passed the bag to another bloke, who emptied it down the nearest drain.

"Come on, who did you buy it off?" Geddes leant over and took him by the scruff of the neck. "Tell me and we'll go easy." He leaned in close. "The last thing we want round here is your type flooding the streets with that poison."

The lad said nothing.

"Don't want to tell me? In that case you're getting a good kicking. That'll teach you to cross us."

The men looked at each other, holding back. None of them were violent as a rule. Geddes had every reason to be angry, but he was taking things too far. The lad lying on the cold concrete wasn't responsible for what had happened to his son.

"We could drag him down to the nick, let them sort it out?" one suggested.

But Geddes was having none of it. He aimed his foot at the boy's stomach and struck out hard with his boot. There was a sharp yelp, followed by coughing as the lad threw up.

"That should teach him. C'mon lads, we've still got work to do," Geddes told the others.

"What if he complains, tells someone?"

Geddes shook his head in disgust. Vigilantes? Carry on like this and they'd soon be a laughing stock. "You lot need to toughen up. You've got these kids scared, don't let that slip."

"We don't need to beat them to a pulp. A short, sharp lesson is all they need. The scum of this town will soon get the message," Wells said.

"You're wrong," Geddes spat. "Give an inch and they'll walk all over you."

"We don't want trouble from the law," Wells whispered. "That lad knows some of us."

"Pack of bloody fairies, that's what you are," Geddes said. "With that attitude you won't frighten anyone. The villains will laugh at you."

"Let the lad go. He's had a thumping. What if he goes to the police?"

"Wouldn't dare," Geddes said. "What's he going to say? That we beat him up for being a druggie! No chance. He'll scuttle off home, lick his wounds and if we've done our job right, think twice before using in future."

He could hear the group muttering as they started to walk away. No one had complained earlier in the pub when he'd laid out exactly what they had to do. *We'll beat the buggers black and blue, that'll teach them.* They'd all agreed, no dissenters.

But out on the streets, with one in their grasp, it was a different matter. Most of them were simply not cut out for it.

Jim Paterson tapped him on the shoulder. He was holding his mobile phone. "Just read on WhatsApp about tools being taken from a shed on Hobson Street. The owner caught the bastard on his CCTV. Take a look?"

The image showed a shadowy figure making off with a holdall. Geddes nodded. "You lot go. I've had enough for one night." He looked round at the others. "Get it right lads. It's up to us — the police are no help. We have to look out for ourselves."

"I know who that is." Another of the group piped up, looking at the grainy image. "He lives in Heron House."

"Okay. Get round there and hang about until he returns." Geddes regarded them. "This is important. The thieving bastards need sorting or they'll take over."

Geddes had said his piece. Giving the lad one last kick, he turned and walked off.

* * *

"I got us a takeaway. Fish and chips do you?" Layla said.

Calladine watched Layla put the food on the warm plates. "Thought we were going for healthy this week?" he queried, tearing off a chunk of fish and squirting brown sauce over it.

"Wait! You're dropping it all over the floor," she shouted at him. "You've got some dreadful habits, d'you know that."

"Sorry, I'm hungry. Need my tea."

"Well, it's this or nowt. You were in late and so was I. I'm not a bloody miracle worker and I presume you're not either. So, for tonight, we make do." As a paramedic with Oldston Ambulance Service, Layla often worked long, unsocial hours.

"Your shift ended over an hour ago. What happened?" The words were out before he could sensor them. They made it sound as if she was responsible for the meals, which, of course, she wasn't.

Calladine held his breath, waiting for the fiery blast, but she let it go. "We attended an incident on the bypass. A teenage girl hit by a car. Fortunately not badly hurt, but she refused to go to the infirmary. By the time we'd convinced her to get checked out, our shift was well over."

"Couldn't you just let her go home, finish on time?"

She was annoyed by his comment. "No, Tom, she had a leg injury, could hardly walk. For all we knew she might have broken something. Best if the doctors take a look."

"Brad Long's had a heart attack. He's in Wythenshawe."

"Oh, that's why you're criticising the food. We'll go back to the diet tomorrow. Fixing him, are they?"

"Apparently so, and I'm not criticising the food."

Layla took a plate of food and sat down by the fire. She looked preoccupied. Something was wrong, and it was down to more than his eating habits.

"Something's up," he said at last. "Whatever it is, out with it. Does no good to let stuff fester."

"It's us. This," she pointed to him and then herself. "Where are we going, Tom? What future does this relationship have?"

That had come out of the blue. He was expecting something more about his eating habits. He looked at her. "Why this? Why now? And do we have to go anywhere? I don't like change, and I thought things were fine as they are."

"Well, they're not," she retorted. "Not for me anyway. You don't seem to notice or even care, but make no mistake, we're in a rut. I have no intention of carrying on like this. I've got the chance of promotion, working with the air ambulance service, but it will mean a move."

Calladine was impressed. "Sounds like a great opportunity. You should grab it."

Layla looked at him. "You don't understand. I'll have to go to Scotland. Inverness to be precise."

Calladine fell silent. That was a fair distance. No chance for any relationship if she moved up there. He didn't want Layla to go, but he had no right to ask her to stay. She'd asked where they were going. That meant she was looking for more than the casual, when-it-suited-them-both relationship they had at present. But anything more serious than that wasn't for him.

"It's your choice," he said. "If I were in your shoes, I'd go for it." He saw her face fall. It wasn't what she wanted to hear.

"It'll mean the end of us," she said. "I'll move away, rarely get back, and become totally wrapped up in my new role."

Calladine sighed. "What do you want from me?"

Layla was upset now, her voice rising. "You shouldn't have to ask. I thought we had a future, but from your response it's obvious I was wrong." She stood up and banged the plate down on the table. "Admit it, I'm just a convenience. Someone to mind the dog and watch your house when you're out."

"It works both ways. As things are, we're okay."

"I'm not after *okay*, Tom. I want more."

The warning bells were going off in Calladine's head. "I'm sorry, Layla, but I'm not the stuff of long-term. Most of my relationships have been short-lived. That's just how it is."

"But it doesn't have to be. Don't you feel *anything* for me?"

She was fast losing patience.

"Of course I do. I like you a lot. We get on well, understand each other and the jobs we do."

"It's not enough. I'm sorry, Tom, but I'm going home. I'll bring Sam back tomorrow." She left her food untouched. Tom heard the front door slam as she left the house.

Calladine hadn't seen this coming. Something had changed, but he'd no idea what or when. He knew what she wanted to hear, but when it came down to it, it wasn't what he wanted.

Suddenly there was a knock at the door. For a moment he thought it might be Layla, coming back. But it wasn't. Another female voice called out, "Mr Calladine!"

Kat Barber. He opened the front door to the tearful woman.

"It's my Sean," she sobbed. "He's been found unconscious and stabbed. They've taken him to the hospital. He was set on by a load of louts. Beat him to a pulp and left him bleeding to death."

CHAPTER 7

Calladine drove Kat Barber to the hospital. She was in no fit state to go alone and her sister was working. She was terrified of seeing what had been done to her son. The idea that he might be permanently disabled, or worse, was torment. Kat knew Sean was thought of as a 'bad boy,' a one-time gang member. But recently he'd seemed better, his moods were more even and he'd kept himself to himself. She sat beside Calladine in the car shaking and sobbing into a hankie.

"I told him not to stay out late. There's all sorts on them streets. It's not safe."

Calladine raised his eyebrows. One of them 'sorts,' as she'd put it, was her own son. "This is Leesdon, there are worse places," he told her. It was true. Nestled up against the Pennine hills, Leesdon was a stone-built village surrounded by lovely scenery. Despite the problematic Hobfield Estate, it was fast becoming a fashionable place to live. It was certainly nothing like neighbouring Oldston. You really had to be careful after dark in that town.

"We've been on our own, me and Sean, since his father left. Sean has no one to look up to. You lot don't do enough. Folk get robbed, beaten up, have their cars trashed, and the police do nothing. Now we've got grown men patrolling the streets happy to lay in to any youngster that crosses their path."

"The vigilantes you told me about last night?"

"Yes, a whole bunch of them. The folk who live in this town are fed up of being let down by you lot. They're not just roughnecks, either. Some local shopkeepers and ordinary working men have joined the group."

"Do you have names, Mrs Barber?"

Kat Barber shook her head. "You know I couldn't tell you, even if I knew. And it's Ms, I never married the bastard who fathered Sean. Anyway, you can call me Kat."

He chanced a smile. "You can drop the 'Mr Calladine' too, my name's Tom."

Calladine pulled into the hospital car park. "I'll come with you. It's violent assault. If Sean's awake, I'll have a word. He might remember who attacked him."

The receptionist told Calladine that Sean was in theatre and to wait. They walked in silence along the corridor to the seating area.

Calladine glanced at Kat as they sat down. She looked tired, which was understandable given that she was worried sick about her son. She was an attractive woman. Calladine put her in her early forties, dark hair in a ponytail, and slim. And she'd known his mother. He wondered if she knew the truth about his parentage? He didn't even know if there'd been rumours. Freda Calladine, who Kat said she'd known, had raised him, but she wasn't his birth mother.

"He will be alright, won't he?" She broke the silence. "I couldn't bear it if he . . . well, you know."

She was shaking. He took her hand. "They'll do their very best, Kat. This is a good hospital."

It was late, a weeknight, and the place was eerily quiet. After a half hour wait, a surgeon walked towards them, his shoes echoing noisily on the tiled floor of the corridor. "Mrs Barber?" he asked.

Kat stood up. "Is he okay? Can I see him?"

Calladine knew from the look on the surgeon's face that it wasn't good.

"I'm very sorry. There wasn't much we could do, I'm afraid. Sean was stabbed in the chest and the blade severed the aorta. He bled out in minutes."

Calladine was shocked. This was murder on a local street. Why hadn't someone phoned him, told him how serious the assault was? Kat Barber looked the surgeon in the eye and then with an almighty wail, dropped to her knees on the floor.

"*Sean!*" she cried out. "He can't be dead. He's my boy!"

Calladine lifted her gently to her feet, helped her to a chair, and put a comforting arm around her shoulder. "I'm so sorry, Kat. I had no idea it was this bad."

"Well, now you do!" she spat back angrily. "There is no law out there anymore. Those men collared my boy and killed him! Murdering scum. They should be strung up!" She pushed Calladine away, her eyes full of hate. "What now, Mr Policeman? Stand by and let this go, will you? Tell us you're not enough resources, that my Sean deserved it because he broke into houses?"

Calladine knew she was in shock, but he was still lost for words. At that moment he heard Rocco's familiar voice.

"Sir! I've just come from the crime scene. I've had the area cordoned off and got forensics on it."

* * *

Rocco was surprised to find Calladine at the hospital. He'd been asked to attend because of the incident involving Sean.

Calladine watched Kat Barber follow the surgeon along the corridor. He was concerned about her, but she had insisted on seeing her son. He turned to Rocco. "She's the lad's mother, and a neighbour of mine. The dead lad broke into my house last night. I thought we'd sorted him out." He shook his head. "Stupid kid. Didn't learn a thing, did he?"

"He was set upon by a group of men," Rocco said. "We've got some CCTV, but they're all wrapped up, scarves, hoods and the like. But uniform thinks one of the group is John Wells, and I agree. He's local, works up at the biscuit factory."

"We'd better talk to him then." Calladine heaved a sigh. "Before we do, I want another word with Kat. Wait here for me." He hurried to catch up with her and the surgeon. He couldn't let her do this on her own. "You have a sister?" He followed her to a window which looked into the side room in which Sean was laid out. "I can get her for you."

"She's working," Kat said with a sob. "Why can't I go in there, hold his hand?"

Calladine knew that Sean would be taken to the morgue and then on to the Duggan. He was a murder victim. There would have to be a forensic post-mortem.

"Because the experts will need to look at him. We want to find who did this."

"They'll cut him up, you mean," she said. "I don't want that! I couldn't bear it. He's my boy!"

Her son lay flat on the bed covered with a white sheet. Despite the tubes still attached to his body, he looked peaceful. The bruising on his face was slight and the blood had been wiped away.

"He looks peaceful, as if he's sleeping." She grabbed Calladine's arm and sobbed on his shoulder.

"Where does your sister work? I'll send a uniformed officer to fetch her for you."

"Buckley Pharmaceuticals," she said. "Our Mandy's on the night shift this week."

Calladine nodded. Buckley's and Alder's employed most folk in the area. Both factories were open twenty-four/seven. What he didn't tell her was that the owner of the pharmaceutical company, Eve Buckley, was his birth mother.

"Mandy won't be able to come. They don't like it if you have too much time off."

"I'll sort it," he said. A quick call to Eve, and Kat's sister could take as much time off as was needed.

"I'm sorry I flew at you," she said. "It's not your fault. You're one of the good ones, I know that."

His face was solemn. "We'll get them, Kat, I promise you. They will pay the price for what they did to Sean."

CHAPTER 8

Day 2

The team sat in silence in the incident room watching the CCTV recording, each pair of eyes intent on the grainy action playing out before them. A group of men giving a lad a good pasting.

"There!" Rocco pointed. "I'm sure that's John Wells."

"How can you tell?" asked Calladine. "Most of his face is covered up."

"He drinks in the Pheasant, sometimes the Wheatsheaf. I've spoken to him a couple of times when I've been in there myself. D'you see that limp? It's due to a nasty fall he had a few months ago, broke his leg badly. I'd know him anywhere."

"Is he normally so violent?" Ruth asked. "That man is giving the lad a right going over."

"That's not Wells." Rocco frowned. "I don't recognise him."

Calladine winced as he watched a boot connect hard with Sean Barber's belly. "The violence is way over the top. Rumour has it that local people are fighting back. They're tired of having no recourse when they get burgled, mugged, or have their cars broken into."

"We attend, do what we can," Alice said.

"It's not enough. How often do we catch one of them, bring them to book? Play that bit of film again," he told Rocco. He watched Sean get a beating, this time in slow motion. "Useful, but we don't see who stabbed him." Calladine sighed. "What about the CCTV after he's beaten?"

"I've had a look but the camera is smashed," Rocco explained. "More than likely by the killer before he struck."

Calladine continued to watch the snippet of film. "It looks like the group move off before he is stabbed. Do we have Sean's mobile?"

"No. Forensics didn't find one," Rocco replied.

"In that case the killer might have taken it. That begs the question — why?"

"Are you saying this could be down to someone else, not one of that group?" Rocco asked.

"I don't know. The street looks empty, but that camera was smashed by someone. We need to know a great deal more about who was there, what part they all played, and where they went afterwards". Calladine said, then addressed the team's admin assistant. "Joyce, can you get on to Sean Barber's phone provider, get the data for us?" He turned back to Rocco. "Any CCTV of the surrounding streets might help. It would give us a clue about who was out and about at the same time."

"We find Wells, lean on him, and he'll tell us what happened," Rocco said. "We have this bit of film and there is bound to be forensic evidence. Wells isn't a criminal, he'll cave under questioning."

They could only hope so. Calladine couldn't rid himself of the feeling that somehow this was his fault. Sean Barber and his mother had haunted him all night. The lad was no angel but he didn't deserve what those men had done to him. He wanted to know the motivation behind it, what they hoped to gain. Granted, Sean was a ruffian, but as far as

Calladine knew, he'd never hurt anyone. Breaking into houses in the dead of night and helping himself was his thing.

"Alice, any joy with the individual known as Street?"

The blonde DC shook her head. "No, sir. I'm going to try the youth club on the Hobfield later. They run an after-school drop-in. Someone there might know him."

"Is this 'Street' important?" Ruth asked.

"I don't know, but Sean Barber did what Street told him. In fact, all the kids do, so I'm told. I want to know what they're up to and what hold he has over them. Plus, Kat Barber told me he encouraged the kids to fight back against the vigilantes. If we're not careful, we could have a full-blown war on our hands. I want this Street found and questioned."

Ruth flopped down into her chair with a sigh. "We're not going to cope, are we? The missing Alder child, and now this. We can only spread ourselves so thin."

Calladine knew she was right, but they could only do their best. An air of gloom had descended on the office. They didn't have a smile between them.

"We'll have Thorpe." He tried to sound upbeat but knew he'd failed when a loud groan went round the room. "Okay, I'll keep him on a tight rein," he gave in. "The rest of you make use of uniform. Alice will look for this 'Street' and find out who else is in his little gang. Rocco, you go after Wells. We want to know who's joined him and what their beef is."

Ruth looked at him. "And me?"

"I want you to get close to Annie Alder and that friend of hers, Joanne. Win their trust. My gut tells me that there's something in the family's background that has led to this kidnap. We'll meet back here before home time, see what we've got."

* * *

Ruth grabbed the Alder file and made herself comfortable. There wasn't much. Statements taken from

Annie and Joanne, and notes made about what the boy, Jack, had told DI Long. Also, the research Rocco had done earlier. She added the email printout and the photo Annie had given her of Sophie. She stopped for a few seconds to study it. Sophie Alder was wearing a party dress and had her blonde hair in plaits. She clutched a blue teddy bear and looked straight at the camera. The toy drew Ruth's attention because it stood out against the cream colour of Sophie's dress.

Ruth's son, Harry, had a favourite soft teddy. A battered old thing he'd had since birth. It had been through the wash a hundred times and was almost threadbare, but Harry loved it. Ruth smiled. Little ones were all the same.

She picked up the office phone and rang Joanne, Annie's friend. She'd speak to her and the boy first. "Sergeant Ruth Bayliss here. Could we meet?" she asked. "I'd also like a chat with Jack if that's possible."

"Jack's my nephew. I take care of him while my sister works part-time. I promised to take him to the soft play centre in Hopecross this afternoon. I don't want to disappoint him."

"That's fine," Ruth said. "I can meet you there. I don't want this to be formal. He's more likely to chat if he gets to know me. I want Jack to tell me what he remembers about that afternoon."

"Jane, my sister, says he's having nightmares." Her voice was sharp. "He's aware Sophie is missing and keeps saying that the witch has taken her."

Ruth frowned. "That's an odd thing to say. I thought he told you a man was standing by the gate? Does Jack now think it could have been a woman?"

"I don't know what Jack thinks. He's a kid, and gets mixed up. He knows talking to strangers is wrong. People bang on about it enough. He's worried. He's aware that Sophie is in some sort of danger. Jack is four now, a bit older than Sophie, and understands more."

"Let's call it a 'getting used to me' session, if you like," Ruth suggested. "No pressure on either of you."

"I'll have a word with Jane first. If she's okay with it, we'll be there about two."

"Who will be with Annie while you're gone? Has our family liaison officer turned up?"

"Yes. Annie sent her packing, I'm afraid. Frankie is with her. She's calmed down and has agreed to be more helpful."

That was something at least.

CHAPTER 9

Calladine would have to speak to Sean's mother. It was not something he was looking forward to. The PM hadn't been carried out yet and she was sure to ask. Forensics would be all over his bedroom. Kat would not relish the intrusion.

"I'm going to see Joanne and her nephew this afternoon," Ruth told him. "I'm hoping the little lad will talk to me. He is our only witness, young as he is. He's now saying that a witch took Sophie. I don't know what to make of it."

"Best of luck. I don't know which is the worse option, you with the kid or me with Kat Barber."

"I thought you said you know her?"

"She's a neighbour, but in a case like this, it doesn't help."

Ruth looked up at him. "What's wrong with you today? I know we're pushed but you've got that face on."

Calladine let out a sigh. "Layla's dumped me. What with everything else, it's a blow I could've done without."

"And you didn't see it coming?"

"Should I have? I thought we were fine."

"You don't get any better, Tom." Ruth shook her head. "She's the commitment type. I knew Layla wouldn't be fobbed off with your weird idea of a relationship for long. You're lucky it lasted all these months."

"I'd no idea she was so into me."

Ruth sighed. "Then again, neither of you are getting any younger. Perhaps she simply saw you as a safe bet."

"Thank you for that." He sniffed. "Remind me not to ask for advice on affairs of the heart from you again!"

Ruth was serious now. "Stop mucking women about, Calladine. Find one you like and then do the right thing."

* * *

Vehicles belonging to the forensics team were parked outside Kat Barber's house. It made finding a free space on the narrow back street difficult. These houses had been here since the last century and the streets were never meant for today's volume of traffic.

Calladine found the front door open. Kat Barber was pacing the sitting room. "They've been up there for hours," she told him. "What are they looking for? My Sean was the one murdered. He didn't do anything."

"It's routine, Kat. I'll go up, see where they're at."

Calladine climbed the stairs and met one of the forensic team on the landing. "Are you done yet? Kat's had enough."

"We've given the lad's room a thorough going over. We'll take his laptop away. And we found this little lot stashed under the floorboards." He held up a clear plastic bag containing a dozen or so wraps. "Cocaine, I reckon. And we found this in one of his drawers." It was a mobile phone.

Sean was a user? Calladine didn't know why he was surprised by that, but he was. He nodded at the mobile. "I want to know what's on that phone pronto."

"There's this little lot, too." The forensics man held up a plastic bag containing jewellery and other valuable small items. "He's been on the rob for a while, I'd say. There's all sorts in here, including some antique silver." He reached into the bag and brought out an object. "These snuffboxes, for example."

"I'm aware Sean was no angel. He even tried to rob me the other night. But I never suspected him of dealing." Calladine sighed and took a closer look at the drugs.

"If that's what it is," the forensics bloke said. "There's not much here. It's the supplier you need to get your hands on."

"Don't say anything to his mother just yet. I'll deal with that one. Take them away and get that laptop looked at. There might be something on it we can use."

Calladine went back down the stairs to speak to Kat. This was going to be tricky. He doubted she had any idea what her son had been up to. "They've found quite a haul. It looks like Sean was making a career of thieving. Sorry, Kat, I know it's not what you want to hear."

"I knew he was up to something, but I was too scared to ask." She folded her arms. "But he was my boy. He didn't deserve to die like that. He met a wrong 'un and I want him found, Tom. I'm trusting you. Don't let me down."

"I will do everything I can." He paused. She looked pale and drawn, probably hadn't slept. Now was not the time to bring up the drugs. "How are you coping? Is your sister staying with you?"

"Yes, thanks for that." She managed a weak smile. "Buckley's have given her time off with pay. Good of them. You must have some influence to pull that one off. Right tight bunch as a rule."

Calladine felt embarrassed. Should he tell her? Why not? Enough people in this town probably knew by now anyway. "Eve Buckley is my birth mother," he admitted after a moment or two.

Kat looked puzzled. "What d'you mean? I thought you were Freda's lad."

"Freda Calladine brought me up from when I was an infant. I knew no different. She never told me the truth about Eve. After Freda died, I found a letter she'd left for me. It told the whole story. My dad and Eve had an affair. I was the result. But Eve was young, unable to support herself, so Frank took me home and Freda raised me as her own."

He inhaled. Talking about his parents brought a lump to his throat.

"Do you see her, Mrs Buckley?"

"Now and then. We have accepted each other, although I think her other son, Simon, isn't keen." Eve had gone on to have two more children, Samantha and Simon.

"Will you inherit some of her money when she's gone?"

Calladine laughed. "I have no idea. We've never discussed it."

"I'd say it's the least she could do. She gave you up. I don't understand how any woman can do that. She should leave you the lot."

"It's not that simple."

"Sorry, I shouldn't pry. And I haven't even offered you a drink."

"I'm fine, Kat. I'll get on. I'll be in touch when we've got something."

Calladine wanted to make further enquiries about the drugs. He wanted to know exactly what Sean had been involved in.

CHAPTER 10

The play centre was busy. It was a half-term afternoon. Ruth spotted Joanne sitting opposite the bouncy castle, watching Jack jump up and down. The noise was off the scale — lots of laughter and screaming kids running around.

"Thanks for coming." Ruth sat down beside her. "Can I get you a coffee or something?"

Joanne shook her head. "I've explained things to Jack," she said. "He's a good boy. He knows what's happened to Sophie isn't right."

"Will he speak to me?"

Joanne nodded. "We can try, but take it slow. It's hit him hard."

She beckoned the boy across to join them. "Jack, this is Ruth. She's the lady I told you about, the one trying to find Sophie."

Ruth gave him a beaming smile. He was slight, with blonde hair. "I bring my little boy, Harry, here. He loves playing on that," she nodded at the bouncy castle. "He's not as big as you so he falls off a lot."

Jack giggled. "I'm going to a party. It's Ellie's birthday."

"Is she having her party here?"

He nodded. "A man is coming to do magic."

"I think I've seen him here before, he's good."

"He gives us a balloon and a present."

"Sounds like fun," Ruth said.

The smile suddenly left Jack's face. "I don't know where they went." He backed off slightly. "I shouted at Sophie to come back but she didn't."

"Who was there, Jack? Who did Sophie run to?"

"The witch. It was the witch who called her. She ran off and left me by the froggy pond. We were looking for frogspawn."

"It's the wrong time of year," Ruth told him. "You should try again in the spring. There'll be lots then."

Jack frowned in concentration. "She wasn't bothered about going with the witch. She waved bye-bye at me."

"Can you remember what the witch looked like, Jack?"

"No!" He ran off.

"See," Joanne said. "He's just not comfortable talking about it."

Ruth thought that he'd seemed perfectly okay with it up until the moment the witch's appearance had come up.

"I'll leave it at that for now," Ruth told Joanne. She turned to look at the boy, who was back bouncing on the castle. "I'm going now, Jack," she called to him. "Will you talk to me again?"

The boy edged a little closer, staring at her. "I don't want to."

Ruth smiled at him. "Tell you what, I'll do you a deal. One more question and that's it."

He nodded.

"Did Sophie know the witch's name?"

He shook his head. "I don't know. But the witch was at the party. The one when Sophie bumped her head."

Jack bounced off and Ruth turned to Joanne, puzzled. "Do you know what he means?"

"No idea. He's a kid. For all we know, he could have dreamt it."

"You mean there was no party? Sophie didn't bang her head?" Ruth asked.

"Not that I can recall. He's confused because there's a party going on here today, and one or two of the kids are dressed up. See." She nodded towards a group of people. "That little girl over there is dressed as a witch."

* * *

Ruth knew very well that children made up stories. Her own son, Harry, did. But Jack had seemed so sure.

"Get anywhere?" Sergeant Thorpe asked her as she entered the incident room.

"If the kid is to be believed, perhaps. But he's four years old and told me that a witch took Sophie."

"That's kids for you." He laughed and leaned back in his chair.

Ruth frowned. "I thought you were up to your eyes in research."

"Nowt to look at. Can't find any 'Street,' and the Alders are whiter than white."

"Look at their private life. There's something, I know it. Annie isn't happy and Rick spends all his time at work."

Much to Ruth's annoyance, Thorpe was constantly checking his watch. As a rule, he didn't stay a second longer than he had to. Calladine wouldn't like that. The team usually worked until they had the case cracked.

"No one admits to knowing this 'Street,' Sarge," Alice announced as she entered the incident room. "I've asked at the youth club and even been round to the school. But they've heard of him. From the furtive looks they gave each other, I could tell that much."

Ruth was pleased. At least Alice had done some work. She was meticulous and had been an asset to the team since joining them as a university student. But why weren't the kids talking? A lad had been killed. "Anything on the vigilantes?"

Alice shook her head. "Not that I'm aware. Rocco has gone off to have a word with one of them. Let's hope he gets more than I did."

* * *

As Calladine was leaving Kat's house, he heard Zoe's familiar voice.

"Dad!" she called. "I could do with a word." She smiled. "Me and Jo have some news."

Zoe Calladine was behind the wheel of her car and had pulled over to speak to him.

"Important, is it?"

"Yes. How about coming to ours after work. Jo will cook and we'll tell you together."

Calladine nodded. "About six, that okay?"

"Don't be late," Zoe instructed as she pulled away.

Calladine had no idea what was going on. Jo Brandon was Zoe's partner. She was an estate agent and had an office on the High Street in Leesdon, where Zoe also worked as a solicitor. He knew they'd been looking at properties together. Perhaps they'd found one at last?

CHAPTER 11

"Drugs?" Ruth asked.

"Several wraps of cocaine." Calladine had told the team what forensics had found once he was back at the station.

"Any clue where it came from?" asked Ruth.

"No, and I haven't told his mum yet. She's enough to think about."

"You're going soft, Calladine," Ruth told him. "Sean Barber had to be involved with some dangerous types. Who d'you think he got the stuff from?"

"It could have been anyone. Leesdon, and the Hobfield in particular, isn't short of dealers."

"Actually, it's gone quiet on that front," Rocco said. "There's been very little dealing recently in the parks or street corners that uniform are aware of."

Ruth shook her head. "It's still going on, that much is certain."

"So what's happened?" Calladine asked. "Why the lull? The usual crew are not clever enough to keep it that quiet." He turned to Rocco. "Are you sure there's been nothing? Uniform not picked anyone up?"

"No, guv, not for dealing. Possession yes, the odd wrap or pill, but nothing major."

"I have to say that Sean Barber didn't strike me as being the type. He wasn't the brightest either. Too easily led."

Calladine wrote this development on the incident board. "Don," he addressed DS Thorpe, "what have you got for us?"

"Nowt, sir. No one admits to knowing this 'Street,' and the Alders are clean."

Calladine stared at him. Thorpe had settled himself in at the spare desk. It was covered in dirty mugs and sandwich wrappers. He hadn't moved all day. "Have you even left the office? Been out there and spoken to anyone?"

"No need to. Alder is as straight as they come. Stands to reason."

How did Long put up with him? "Off your arse, Sergeant, and do some real work for a change. I want this putting to bed. We've a missing kid and the answer lies with her family. My gut tells me that much."

"Where do you suggest I try? The biscuit factory?"

"No. Richard Alder is publicity shy. Find out what pub the workers use and get in there. Chat to them, find out what they think of Alder."

Calladine saw the grin on Thorpe's face and was quick to set him straight. "That's not permission to get bladdered, Sergeant, keep that in mind."

"When is the Barber PM scheduled?" Ruth asked.

"I'm hoping tomorrow. Get it out of the way for Kat's sake."

"Do you want me to talk to her?"

"No. Leave Kat Barber to me," Calladine said firmly. "Okay, back to work everyone."

* * *

"You like her, don't you?" Ruth said later on as they were leaving.

Calladine didn't reply. He knew she meant Kat Barber.

"I know you do. She lives round the corner from you for a start."

"She's a neighbour, even knew my mum. Freda," he added hurriedly, "not Eve."

"Like I said, you like her."

"She's just lost her son, for Heaven's sake. Whether I like her or not is immaterial." He paused. "But yes, Kat's okay."

"And Layla?"

Calladine exhaled deeply. "It's over. She's fed up with me. Said as much. Told me she's moving to Inverness."

Ruth was surprised. "Really? You'll miss her."

He shrugged.

"You're a piece of work, d'you know that?"

Calladine was well aware of his faults. He watched Ruth walk towards her car. Her relationship with Jake wasn't all sweetness and light. They'd had problems. But she'd stuck at the relationship, made Jake see that what they had was worth fighting for.

"Tom!" A female voice called out. "I hoped I'd catch you."

Just what he needed, another of his exes. "Monika!" He was surprised. Despite living in the same town, they usually avoided each other. He wondered what had changed

"This isn't a social call," she said at once. "I have a problem and hope you can help."

Calladine tried a smile, but inside he groaned. Spend too much time with Monika and he'd be late for Zoe.

"What's happened?"

"I'm not sure."

"Well, if you don't know what the problem is, how am I supposed to help?"

"Do you fancy a drink? Perhaps the Wheatsheaf?"

It wasn't a bad idea. As long as Monika was being straight with him. They had history. A couple of years ago they had been thinking of marriage. The pair had been together for a long time. But then Calladine had been swept off his feet by another woman. He'd dumped Monika and she'd never forgiven him. Not that he blamed her. Ruth was right, he was a piece of work.

"I'd better ring Zoe first, tell her I'll be late," he smiled.

"Is she still with that American woman?"

"Jo? Yes. The pair of them are making a go of it. Doing well, too."

CHAPTER 12

The Wheatsheaf was almost empty. That suited Calladine —
he didn't want tongues wagging about the pair of them. He
and Monika ordered their drinks at the bar and then took a
table by the fire.

"You're looking good." She smiled at him. "Your new
girlfriend knocking you into shape?"

Calladine decided against telling Monika that Layla had
left him. "She's trying, but it's a slog, I can tell you." She
was looking at him expectantly. "You look okay, too," he
mumbled. He didn't want Monika getting any ideas. Their
relationship was well and truly over.

"We've expanded the business recently," Monika said.
"We get out into the community more, care for folk in their
own home. You know the sort of thing, we offer visits by
carers for those who need us. It helps to keep the elderly
independent for longer."

Calladine saw the sense in this. Monika had successfully
run a care home in Leesdon for a number of years. She was
the manager and part-owner and knew the business inside out.

"Consequently, we are getting to know a lot more of the
local elderly folk and they speak to us, tell us what's going

on. One of them, Rowena Hargreaves, is giving me cause for concern."

Calladine was puzzled. "The aged are not my area of expertise, Monika. My experience with the elderly is limited to my mother, Freda. I'm sure there must be someone better qualified you can speak to."

"Shut up and listen, Tom. I haven't finished yet," she snapped at him. "You're just the same as ever, too quick to jump to conclusions!" Outburst over, she took a breath and composed herself. "I think this is important, and something you need to hear. Rowena was admitted to hospital last week. She was very poorly."

"The elderly get ill. I can't do anything about that."

Monika glared at him. "Rowena was ill because she had overdosed on drugs and had been drinking heavily."

"Freda liked a gin," he shrugged. "On occasions, I've known her be a bit worse for wear."

"Will you please take this seriously. Rowena is eighty-nine years old, Tom. She'd taken cocaine and pills — ecstasy the doctors tell me. She's lucky to be alive."

She had Calladine's attention now. "Could she have taken them by mistake?"

"I doubt it. For starters, where would she get the stuff from? I've wracked my brain and can find no explanation. I went to her house when she was first referred to us. She was independent, and mostly fended for herself. Her home was neat, everything in its place. We attended for several weeks in the beginning and then Rowena asked us not to go anymore. No reason given, other than she could see to herself. Then she ended up in hospital. I went back to her house to arrange for it to be prepared for her return. The place was an absolute state. It looked as if a herd of elephants had trampled through her home. She had a cabinet full of porcelain figurines and small silver items. Stuff that belonged to her parents. They've gone, too."

"You think she sold the items to buy drugs?"

"Don't be stupid! I think she was robbed! Who the culprit is, I've no idea. But what puzzles me more is where the drugs came from."

"The theft has to be down to someone she knew, someone who went to the house regularly and got to know what she had."

Monika gave Calladine a hard look. "We are the only people who have visited her in a while. I hope you're not suggesting that one of my care workers is robbing the clients?"

Calladine hadn't meant her to take it that way. "No, that's not what I'm saying." He paused. "But you have looked at all your staff, vetted them thoroughly?"

Monika got to her feet, frowning. "I should have known I'd get nowhere with you."

"I'm sure there's a simple explanation, Monika. I'm simply throwing a few ideas around, that's all."

"I have a bad feeling, Tom. Something is going on in this town. I can't put my finger on it, but things aren't right. The drugs are the real issue here. You must see that. Rowena is nearly ninety. She is no drug user, believe me."

Calladine's thoughts were on Sean Barber and what forensics had found in his bedroom. Perhaps Sean was involved somehow.

"Is there anyone who would recognise the missing items, if they're found?"

"There are some photos that were taken for insurance purposes. I could get them if you think it'd help."

"Do that. Drop them into the station."

"You know something, don't you?" She was looking at him. "You forget, I know you, Tom. I can spot the signs. You might sound all disinterested, but you've got your detective head on."

"For now, it's just a theory, Monika. Don't go jumping to conclusions."

"I'll bring the photos in tomorrow. And I'll expect to be kept informed. I promised Rowena I'd do my best to get her stuff back."

"Let me see those photos first, then we'll see."

* * *

Rocco had been chasing John Wells for most of the day. He wasn't at home or at the biscuit factory. Nor was he at the Wheatsheaf, as Rocco had hoped. His wife was no help — she had no idea where he'd gone. Rocco decided to give it one last shot. He'd try the Pheasant on the Hobfield.

The Hobfield estate was the last place on earth Rocco would choose to go. He was well aware of its reputation and had been badly injured on the deck of one of the tower blocks in the past. He'd received a bang on the head which had nearly put paid to his career.

"They're not keen on the law around here. You'd better wait outside," he told the uniformed officer who'd been with him all day. "If I'm not out in ten, come and find me."

Rocco knew that seeing a police uniform in this pub would cause a riot. It was with some trepidation that he walked through the door. A quick glance around and he spotted Wells. He was propping up the bar, a pint in his hand.

"John," he said affably. "Could do with a word."

John Wells gestured to a table in the corner. "Make it quick. You're not the type to be seen with, not round here."

"Where were you last night?" Rocco began, once they were seated.

"Why? What are you pinning on me now?"

"Nothing. It's a simple enough question."

"I was at home with the wife."

"Not patrolling the streets with your mates beating up young lads then?"

"What d'you take me for?" he said.

"You're telling me you're not one of the vigilantes?"

"You're way off beam there, copper. Too busy working, that's me. I've got no time for that lark. But good luck to them, that's what I say. Mate of mine was broken into last week. You lot did nowt. Another mate lost his son. The bastards plied him with drink and drugs. Lad wasn't the full shilling to start with. By the time those idiots finished with him he didn't know what he was doing."

"Your mates reported all this?" Rocco asked.

Wells scowled at him. "Pointless. Geddes got so far then met a brick wall. In the end he wrote to the coroner."

"You see, John, we have CCTV which shows a group of men giving a lad a thumping. One of them has a limp, very much like yours."

"No, you've got that wrong. Can you see my face?"

Rocco shook his head.

"There you are then," he grinned. "Come back when you've got real proof. Until then, do one, copper."

Rocco got to his feet. Wells was right, they didn't have anything concrete. Time to play his final card. "We'll soon have forensic evidence, John. For your sake, I hope none of it points to you. That lad wasn't simply beaten, he was stabbed to death. This is a murder inquiry."

Wells' face went pale. "A pasting, yes, the little sod was carrying drugs. But that's as far as it went."

"What are you saying now, John? Were you there or not?"

"Yes, but so were the others. And no one stabbed him," he insisted. "None of us had a weapon. That was made clear from the start. No one was supposed to carry."

Rocco sat back down and passed him a notebook and pen. "I want their names."

Wells dutifully wrote them down. "He were hurt, yes. We left the lad groaning on the ground. The we came back here. Some thieving little git had taken tools from a garage round the back of yon tower block."

"All of you came back together?"

Wells looked up from the notebook. "Bill Geddes stayed behind. Said he'd had enough, wanted to get home."

* * *

"You look done in." Zoe said, opening her front door. "Don't you ever think you're getting a bit old for this lark, dad?"

"No, never." Calladine followed her into the kitchen. Whenever this topic came up in conversation, which it did frequently, he always tried to swerve it. "What else would I do? The job is my life, Zo."

She smiled at him. "Poor you. Chasing criminals and low life isn't my idea of fun."

"Anyway, sorry I'm late," he said, changing the subject. "Monika of all people wanted a word. We had a quick drink. I didn't have much choice — you know how she gets."

Jo, Zoe's partner, a smartly dressed, dark-haired woman, joined them. She put a protective arm around Zoe's waist and they grinned at him. It was obvious that something was up.

"Come on then, you pair. Whatever it is you want to tell me is obviously good news. What is it?"

They looked at one another and then back at Calladine. "We're having a baby," Zoe announced. "You're going to be a grandad!"

CHAPTER 13

Day 3

"I've got a list of the vigilantes who were on the streets the night Barber was killed. Wells told me that a man called." Rocco took a moment to check his notes. "Bill Geddes was the last to leave. He was left alone with Barber still very much alive and writhing on the ground."

"Geddes?" Calladine queried.

"We know that name," Ruth said. "Wonder if it's the same man Natasha mentioned when we saw her. The one asking for a second PM on his son."

"Bring him in," Calladine told Rocco. "Street?" he asked, turning to Alice.

"Still nothing, sir, but the kids know him. Won't admit anything though."

"We'll wait and see what Sean's phone data yields. We found a second one hidden with the drugs in his bedroom. I'm hoping it's the one he used to contact the dealer."

Rocco looked dubious. "If this is a serious operation then you'll get very little. The gang will use burner phones, disposable, prepaid ones, not their own."

"We've searched Barber's room and didn't find any," Calladine said. "But we'll keep it in mind."

He turned to Ruth. "Did you get anywhere with the boy?"

"A witch took Sophie." She rolled her eyes. "The one at the party when Sophie bumped her head. I intend to have a word with Annie about that shortly."

Calladine's gaze strayed to the empty spare desk. "Does anyone know what's happened to Thorpe?"

"You sent him to do research in a pub, what d'you expect?" Ruth offered. "I don't think he'll be in any time soon."

"He'd better have something bloody good to show for his efforts when he does turn up. In the meantime, I've had a summons from Richard Alder. He's demanded to see me this morning."

"We don't have much to tell him," Ruth cautioned. "I doubt he'll be pleased."

"Once you've spoken to Annie, text me the gist," he said. "Rocco, round up Bill Geddes and his vigilante mates and keep them here until I get back. I want a word with Geddes."

He turned to one of the uniformed officers. "A woman called Monika Smith might call in asking for me this morning. With luck she'll have some photos of stolen items. Will you see to her if I'm not back?"

The officer nodded.

"That back on, is it?" Ruth teased.

"No!" he replied. "She met me after work last night. She wanted to talk to me about an elderly woman they look after. I'm waiting until I know more, but it could be a piece of this puzzle we're working on."

"The Alder kidnapping?"

"No, the other one. Sean and the drugs."

Calladine waited until the others had left the office and he was alone with Ruth. "Zoe's pregnant," he said. "Her and Jo told me the news last night."

Ruth chuckled. "Grandad it is then. You'll need to polish up your skills, you know — feeding, changing nappies, walks in the park, the job lot."

"I never had any of those skills to begin with. I didn't have a hand in raising Zoe, remember. I didn't even know she existed until just before Freda died." He sat down beside Ruth. "To be honest, I'm stunned. I'd no idea they wanted kids. I mean . . . how does that even work? Her and Jo are both women!"

"They go for IVF and get a donor. It costs a bit, but I imagine they can afford it. It's no biggie, these days, Tom. Lots of same-sex couples have families. How far gone is she?"

But it was a biggie for Calladine. He'd barely got used to being a father to Zoe. "Twelve weeks. The next scan should reveal if it's a boy or a girl."

"I bet they're both excited. Do they know anything about the donor? A single friend of mine did something similar and was able to choose hair colour and all sorts of attributes."

Calladine thought for a moment. "To be honest, I never thought to ask."

"In that case, it could be someone they know. Have you considered that one?" She raised an eyebrow and smiled.

"Keep this to yourself for now, Ruth. I'm not ready for all the 'grandad' jibes just yet."

* * *

Ruth and Alice walked up the drive of the Alder house. "Weigh her up," Ruth told Alice, "I'd like your first impressions. We think something odd is going on, but it's a guessing game, I'm afraid."

"Isn't it simply a case of the Alders being distraught because their child is missing? I don't have any kids of my own, but I doubt my behaviour would be in any way normal, if it was me."

"Call it gut instinct, then," Ruth smiled. "Both me and Calladine have a real dose of it. Something's not right with this one. I'd value your input."

Once again it was Frankie who answered the door. "Found the kid yet?" she asked straight off. The young woman slouched against the door, arms folded. "Course you haven't, bloody useless the lot of you," she said.

Ignoring the remark, Ruth asked, "Is Annie up to talking?"

"See for yourself." Frankie nodded towards the woman indoors, who was staring out of the back window.

"I blame myself," she said as the two detectives approached. "You were right to ask what Joanne and I had been doing. I should have paid more attention to the little ones outside. Instead, I was laughing, joking, and swigging wine as if I didn't have a care in the world."

"Annie, can DC Bolshaw and I ask you a few more questions?" Ruth asked.

With a heavy sigh, Annie turned and flopped onto a sofa. "Ask away."

Ruth and Alice sat down opposite her. Annie looked pale and tired. But more alarming was the large bruise on her left cheekbone.

"How did that happen?" Ruth asked gently.

"It's nothing. I fell against the sideboard."

Ruth doubted that. Annie couldn't meet her gaze. Something was definitely wrong. But it was no use pushing her. Annie was unlikely to tell them, particularly if the injury was her husband's handiwork.

"Within the last few weeks did Sophie go to a party, perhaps in fancy dress, for example?"

Annie shook her head. "What's this about parties? Is it important?"

"It could be," Ruth said. "You're quite sure? A birthday party for one of her friends, perhaps? At the event Sophie might have fallen and bumped her head."

"I've told you, no!" Annie snapped. "We haven't been to any parties since Christmas last year."

"Was the little boy, Jack, there?"

"Didn't you hear me!" Annie stood up and went back to the window, her back to them. "No parties! Have you got that?"

"You're sure you haven't forgotten? Perhaps an event that a child might think was a party. The little boy Jack was there and some people were in fancy dress."

Annie frowned. "No. I want you to go now. I've had enough of this. I can't do with all these questions. I'm not well."

"Jack was the last person to see Sophie," Ruth explained. "I know he's a child but he says that it was someone he saw at a party who took Sophie. He said it was the same party where your little girl fell and bumped her head."

"He's talking rubbish."

Annie Alder sounded adamant, but there was confusion on her face. Ruth was equally sure that Annie knew very well what she was on about, but for reasons of her own wouldn't tell them.

"Have you received any more emails, Mrs Alder?" Alice asked.

"No." Annie felt at the bruise on her cheek. "I want you to go now. I'm tired."

"Okay," Ruth agreed, "but we'll talk again."

The two detectives left Annie and made their way back along the hallway. "She's lying," Alice whispered. "I see what you mean now. I think there is something iffy going on."

"Piss off the pair of you, did she?" Frankie Halliwell stood by the front door. "She's good at that just lately. She's pissed lover boy off big-style too. Who'd have thought it? Just goes to show, you can't rely on anyone."

"Do you recall Sophie going to a party recently?" Alice asked her.

"No. But then I wouldn't, would I. Keep away from little family get-togethers as a rule. Safer that way."

"What d'you mean, Frankie?" Ruth asked.

"Only that it's better to keep out of his way. Rick hasn't got time for anyone these days, never mind parties."

"Business that good, eh?" Ruth said.

Frankie Halliwell gave her a funny look. "He's raking it in, that's for sure. But I'm not sure it's all down to that factory of his."

Ruth was about to ask her what she meant when Annie interrupted. She looked furious.

"You'd be wise to keep your nose out, Frankie," she shouted from the doorway. "Get in here and stop gossiping. I want you to help me with something."

Ruth was curious but decided to let it drop. "Bye for now," Ruth said as they left.

"What d'you think she meant?" Alice asked Ruth once they were outside. "If Richard Alder's money isn't down to the biscuit factory, then where is he getting it from?"

Ruth looked thoughtful. "I think we should make that question a priority."

CHAPTER 14

The biscuit factory offices were housed in the new building. The set up was impressive. Looking at the décor and office furniture, Calladine could see that no expense had been spared. Testament that Alder had put his Hobfield roots well and truly behind him. Coming from his family, that couldn't have been easy.

Calladine was shown straight up to Alder's office.

"Found my daughter yet?" he barked as the detective entered the room. Alder was sitting at his desk, and, despite the early hour, a glass of whiskey was in his hand. Giles Pennington, his new friend, was pacing the room. There was an atmosphere, as if Calladine had interrupted a heated argument between the two men.

Richard Alder had changed a lot since Calladine had known the family a few years ago. Back then Richard had been the skinny, small one. Now he was tall and had filled out. He still had the mop of blonde hair that had made him stand out as a teenager.

"You're running out of time. You lot are dragging your feet. You don't seem to realise how serious this is." Alder tossed a piece of paper at him. "Arrived by email within the last hour. It pulls no punches. He's asking for a million or we don't see Sophie again. I've updated your DCI Birch."

"I hope you people have a plan," Pennington said stonily.

Calladine glanced at the man and then sat down on the chair opposite Alder. Whoever Pennington was, he wasn't local. Folk brought up around Leesworth had a distinct northern accent. Pennington's was too bland. He was a tall man with short dark hair. His clothes were expensive. Pennington looked like the archetypical businessman, but Calladine wasn't taken in. There was something of the crook about him.

Calladine took a few moments to study the text. Just a few words and to the point. The abductor had played his hand — a million pounds for the safe return of the child. But there were no instructions.

"You will get at least one further communication," came Calladine's considered reply. "An email or a phone call telling you how they want the money delivered."

Alder gave a hollow laugh. "Let's hope they don't want it in cash. That would give the bank in Leesdon a panic attack."

Calladine frowned. "You must not pay anything without our say-so. Do you understand? And don't tell the press anything else. We'll make a statement in due course. Excess publicity will make the abductor jittery, and he may do your child harm."

"Richard wants his daughter back. What is he supposed to do, wait for you to act?" Pennington smiled smugly. "To date you have achieved nothing. At least this way, Sophie comes back to us."

"If it was up to me, I wouldn't have involved you at all." Alder was angry now. "It was Annie who did that. The silly bitch doesn't know what she's doing half the time."

Calladine was taken aback. More evidence of a shaky marriage. "This isn't a domestic drama, sir. Your daughter is in real danger unless we find her soon. Your wife did the right thing. You need us, and my advice is don't hand any money over. What's stopping whoever took your child from grabbing the ransom and running without giving Sophie back? You have no guarantees. Have you told Annie about the demand?"

Alder ran a hand over his face. "This is a mess." He swallowed the rest of the whiskey in one go. "All Annie has to do is take care of her. She can't even manage that properly." He shook his head. "She doesn't know about the demand. And you don't tell her — understood? It'd finish her."

"We'll do our best."

Alder buried his face in his hands and started to weep. "Find her, please. You have to bring her home. If anything happens to Sophie, it will kill us both."

"I will send one of our technical team round to look at your computer. They will look at the IP address the email was sent from, and other information." At that moment Calladine heard his phone beep. He took it from his pocket. It was a message from Ruth. She told him that Annie could not recall a children's party.

Despite the state Alder was in, he had to ask. "Mr Alder, do you remember Sophie attending a party recently? She may have fallen, bumped her head?" He gave the man a few moments to think. "It may have been fancy dress."

"Sorry. I work long hours. Sophie could have gone to a friend's birthday party, I just don't know. Annie is the one to ask."

"No matter. It is something that has come up, that's all."

"What do I do now, Inspector? Apart from go slowly mad that is?"

"Stay alert and the moment you get anything else you contact me." Calladine handed him a card. "Do not do anything on your own. You do that and you risk Sophie's life." He paused. Alder was not handling this well. "Do you have any idea at all who might have done this?"

Alder stared back at the detective, his eyes bright with rage. "Do you imagine I'd be sitting here wallowing over a whiskey if I did?"

There was no doubting how cut up Alder was about his daughter's abduction. Calladine's observations of the man made him believe that Alder's reaction rang true. On his way back to the car, Calladine spotted Billy Alder in one of the firm's garages. He'd have to speak to him too. He was family.

"Billy!" Calladine shouted. "A word."

Billy Alder was nothing like his younger brother. He didn't have Richard's style or looks. Where Richard wore a suit, Billy was dressed in jeans and overalls, and had oil on his hands.

"I didn't realise you worked here, Billy."

"Kind of him, don't you think? I ask my brother for work and he sticks me in there." He nodded at the workshop. "We service all the lorries, and keep the company vehicles on the road."

"It's work, Billy. Keeps you out of trouble."

"He's having a laugh," Billy sneered. "Likes to lord it over everyone. But folk aren't fooled. He's got the Hobfield running through him just as we all have. Can't shake your roots."

"You know about Sophie going missing?"

Billy nodded. "Bad business."

"When did you last see her?"

"To be honest, I can't remember. He might be my brother, but we don't socialise. Likes to keep me in my place, does Rick." At that moment there was a loud crash from the workshop. "Got to go, place falls apart if I don't keep an eye on those idiots."

* * *

Ruth had a hunch. Annie was such a worrier that it was possible she'd sought medical help if Sophie had indeed bumped her head. Back at the nick, Ruth phoned an old friend, Doc Hoyle. Sebastian Hoyle had been the senior pathologist attached to Leesworth hospital. Since retirement, he'd worked part-time as a locum. Ruth hoped he'd be able to help them.

"It's a long shot, but I have to find out if a child was seen either in A&E or the walk-in centre within the last few weeks. It will have been for a bump on the head. I don't need details, just a yes or no will do."

The doc pursed his lips. "I will need the consent of a parent, Ruth. You know how this works. As much as I appreciate what you're trying to do . . ."

"I know, I know," she sighed. "Now I feel bad for asking. Let me get back to you. I'm sure no one is going to object." She paused for a moment. "Perhaps you could have the answer ready for next time I call? The child's name is Sophie Alder."

Ruth's instincts told her that Annie wouldn't give her consent. She rang Calladine.

"Are you still with Alder?" she asked.

"I was just about to leave. Why?"

"Ask him to ring the doc and give his permission for him to tell us if Sophie was treated for a bang on the head recently."

"Is it important?"

"I think so."

Half an hour later, Doc Hoyle rang her back.

"Lucky for you I know Rick Alder. I've met him at the cricket club a couple of times. He's happy for me to give you any information there is."

"And?" Ruth asked, impatient after the wait.

"Sophie was seen in A&E a fortnight ago. The doctor who dealt with her said the child was dressed up in one of those princess dresses the kids find so appealing."

"Was the bump a bad one?"

"No. It was a case of a panicking parent, nothing more."

CHAPTER 15

Calladine arrived back at the station to find Ruth and Alice sifting through a pile of photos.

"Monika dropped these off," Ruth said. "Why are they so important?"

"There's an elderly woman that Monika's care home sees to. The woman had a number of silver items stolen. Given what we found in Sean Barber's room, she might get some of them back."

"How was Alder?" she asked.

"Gutted. What about Annie?"

"I'm not sure. Annie said she didn't recall the party but the doc said it was only a fortnight since Sophie was treated for the bump to her head. And she was wearing fancy dress." She walked over and tapped the incident board. "I'm wondering why Annie's behaviour is so off-beam for the mother of a kidnapped child. Why didn't she simply tell us the truth? Also, she's got a nasty bruise on her cheek."

Calladine frowned. "Did she say how she got it?"

"Only the usual story — she tripped."

"Has she received any more emails?" he asked.

"No."

"Well, Richard Alder has received a demand for a million," Calladine said. "He hasn't told his wife. We keep that close for the time being."

Alice looked shocked. "Does he have a million to hand over?" she asked. "Frankie thinks all his money comes from the factory. She might have said more, but Annie stopped her."

"Like I've said before, Alder's factory is a damn good business," Calladine reminded them.

"Okay, forget the money for a moment," Ruth said. "Why is Annie being so selective in what she tells us?"

"Could she be having an affair?" Alice suggested. "That might be where the bruise came from. Her husband finds out and lamps her one."

"I doubt it," Ruth said.

"Don't rule anything out," Calladine told them as Rocco entered the room.

"I've got three of the vigilantes downstairs including Bill Geddes. I reckon he's worth leaning on, guv. He's angry about something. It's oozing from every pore. He flies off the handle at the least provocation."

"Good work, Rocco. You and I will speak to him shortly." Calladine turned to Alice. "Have a go at matching the items in the photos with the haul we brought in from Sean Barber's bedroom," he said. "Then you and Ruth have another go at Annie Alder. If you ask me, she knows damn well who took her daughter."

"What about her friend, Joanne? She might know something," Alice suggested.

"No. Go straight to Annie. Push hard enough and she'll crack. She's afraid of something. Don't tell her about the ransom demand, but do threaten to tell her husband that she's been less than honest with us."

* * *

Bill Geddes sat in the interview room with a uniformed officer for company. He did not look well. And he was jumpy.

"Whatever it is, I can't help," he said as Calladine sat down opposite him.

"I think you can," Calladine said firmly. "You and your mates set about a lad the other night. Gave him a right beating." Calladine saw Geddes' eyes slide away. He had guilt written all over his face.

"The little gits need teaching a lesson. They rob and vandalise and no one lifts a finger, particularly not you lot."

"You're an angry man, Mr Geddes. Was it you who finished him off? Waited for the others to leave and then stabbed him to death?"

Calladine saw the man's eyes widen with horror. "What d'you take me for!" he blustered. He half rose to his feet and leant forward. "A bit of rough stuff, teach the lad a lesson. But that's as far as it went. All the group want is a bit of peace and quiet round here. The thieving bastards are taking over, and they don't care who gets hurt. But retaliate, take them on, and it's a different story. Gets your attention then."

"The lad is dead, Mr Geddes," Calladine said soberly. "Someone killed him. You and your mates were there, and you were the last to leave."

Geddes slumped back into his chair. "He were fine when I left."

"Why did you leave the others? The night's work wasn't over, I believe."

"After laying into the lad I realised I hadn't the stomach for it," he admitted. "True, I wanted to make the bastards pay for what they did to my boy, but I'm not a violent man. I threw a few punches. I don't deny that, but I'm no killer."

"You do a pretty good impression, Mr Geddes."

"What would you know! I wanted to kill the kids who did that to Alex, but I can't, I don't have it in me. I realised that after I'd nearly kicked that lad half to death."

Was Geddes telling the truth? Time to change tactic. "Tell me what happened to your son."

"Talking about Alex hurts. You have to understand, this isn't easy. There was just me and him."

79

"Tell me what you can. I want to understand."

Geddes relaxed a little. "Alex wasn't like most lads his age. He was autistic, for a start. He has always struggled and raising him was no picnic, believe me. He didn't make friends easily, preferred his own company. He wasn't too bright either. He was always in trouble at school for not doing his work. The time I spent trying to get him help — but it came to nothing in the end. Earlier this year a group of local lads took him under their wing. Dragged him around with them for months. When I saw who they were I knew no good would come of it. A couple of them were off the Hobfield, and that Barber kid was another."

Calladine looked at the man in surprise. "You're telling me that Sean Barber, the lad who was knifed, was one of the group who went around with your Alex?"

"Yes. Him and the others kept going round to Alex's flat, making a noise, disturbing the neighbours. I told him, carry on like this and you'll get thrown out. I'd worked hard, badgered the council for months to get him that place. I wanted to prepare him for the future, make him independent, you see. He won't always have me to sort him out. After his death I had to clean up. The place was in a right state. Those kids had all but trashed it."

"Did you find anything hidden there, Mr Geddes. Drugs, for example?"

Geddes shook his head. "No. But then I wasn't looking."

"Give us the address. Our forensics people will take a look."

Bill Geddes nodded, then continued, "This summer, they all went to that concert up on the Clough. Alex wasn't keen, but he went along anyway. By then I think he was already addicted and afraid to stand up to them in case they cut off his supply. Their hold on him was just too strong to shake. At the concert they plied Alex with booze, fed him pills and cocaine. Probably for a laugh, that's what they were like. But this time Alex had a bad reaction. The stewards at the event called an ambulance but he died in hospital later that day."

Geddes was visibly upset.

"That was a terrible thing to happen," Calladine said. "But those lads weren't to know that Alex would react so badly. It was deemed to be accidental death, I believe?"

"It were no accident!" Geddes spat. "They knew those pills were dodgy. Used my boy as a bloody guinea pig."

"Do you have any proof of that?"

"Course I bloody don't! None of them will talk to me and you lot did nowt."

Calladine took a breath. "I'm aware that you've asked for a second post-mortem. What is it you think they will find?"

"Marks on his body that will prove they hurt him in some way. They were using Alex. I don't know what for, but he wouldn't have been with those lads unless they had something on him or were using physical violence."

Calladine considered this. Alex Geddes had been a vulnerable young man. Why would lads like Sean Barber and the others even be interested? What was it they were after? If it was just about having a laugh, they'd have got bored pretty quickly. But according to Geddes, Alex had been plagued by them for a while.

"I can't promise anything, Mr Geddes, but I will try and get that post-mortem for you."

Geddes nodded. "What about the lad who died? Still think I did it?"

"That lad was Sean Barber. You have just told me that he was one of the lads who tormented your son. You do have a motive, Mr Geddes. Do you still have the clothes you were wearing that night?"

Geddes frowned. "Yes. Why?"

"I'll send someone round for them. They will have to go to the lab. For your sake, let's hope we don't find any of Sean Barber's blood on them."

CHAPTER 16

"Sean Barber's phone data is in," Joyce told Calladine when he returned to the incident room. "Sent through by the provider, from the mobile lost at the scene." She handed him several sheets of paper.

"Has the phone turned up yet?"

"No, sir, the provider says it is turned off. They'll monitor it, and when it's turned on again, they'll let us know."

Calladine scanned the list. "There are dozens of numbers on here." He handed the sheets back. "Check them out will you, Joyce. They could well be the numbers of friends, family — that one is definitely his mother." He pointed to a number. "Anything odd amongst this lot, let me know."

"What about his internet history?" Alice suggested.

"There's nothing on the list," Joyce told her. "I did query that. But the provider assured me that all he used the phone for was calls and texts. Unusual, but there you are."

"We've got his laptop. That might give us something."

Joyce nodded. "I'll push the techie for the data on that. Any social media accounts he had might be interesting."

"Geddes says he didn't stab Sean. I believe him." The others looked at Calladine in surprise. "True, he had a motive. But he's a ruffian, not a killer. Get uniform to accompany him back to his house and pick up the clothes he was wearing the night Sean was stabbed. Get them to the Duggan and tell them to look for blood traces." He looked thoughtful. "I bet they don't find any."

"If not Geddes, then who?" Ruth asked.

"A rival gang perhaps. Don't worry, we'll get there. Thorpe not shown his face yet?"

Heads shook around the room. Calladine picked up his phone and rang the sergeant. "Where the hell are you, Don? We haven't seen you in hours."

"Staking out the Alder gaff on the Hobfield, sir. Alf and Billy are both at home. There's been a lot of coming and going. Young kids mainly. They've definitely got some scam going on."

"What age?" Calladine wondered if they were the same teenagers who'd been setting up the drug dens.

"Kids, no more than twelve years, I'd say."

"They'll be part of his football team. Billy coaches them. Any sign of the missing child, Sophie Alder?"

"No, sir."

"Has he left the flat much, seen anyone?"

"He went to the offy for booze, that's all."

"Did you speak to Richard Alder's employees?"

"A few. No one had a bad word to say about him. The perfect employer, as far as they are concerned."

"Okay. Get back to the nick before five to report back."

"There is something else that will interest you, sir," Thorpe said quickly before Calladine could hang up. "Billy Alder had that Halliwell girl trailing in his wake when he came back from the offy. It looked like they'd had a right set-to. Screaming at him, she was, but I couldn't hear what it was about."

"Frankie?"

"That's the one."

Calladine hung up and looked at Ruth. "Alder's older brother Billy and Frankie Halliwell have been seen arguing. What d'you make of that?"

"They're bound to know each other. Frankie was brought up on the Hobfield too, don't forget."

"Check where she lives. I fancy having a word with that young woman."

Ruth nodded, but she wasn't really listening anymore. Her attention was on the photo of Sophie Alder, the one of the little girl in her party dress. She was comparing it with the photo on the email sent by the abductor.

"Alice, what d'you see on these?"

Alice ran critical eyes over both pictures. "Different clothes. Can't tell where either was taken, but that toy is the same, the blue teddy."

"Exactly! I'm kicking myself now for not noticing it before. It's the same toy in both photos, but that can't be. Annie said the kids didn't take any toys outside." Ruth picked up her phone and tapped in Joanne's number. She had to double-check.

"DS Bayliss here," she said when Joanne picked up. "A quick question for you. When Jack and Sophie went outside that day, did they take any toys with them to play with?"

"No," Joanne replied immediately. "It'd been raining. Annie said they could play hide and seek or football. Toys would've got wet and muddy."

"You're quite sure about that?"

"Yes. Why, is it important?"

"Just clearing something up. Thanks, Joanne." Ruth didn't want Joanne relaying her fears to Annie.

"No toys were taken outside," Ruth told Alice. "So how come Sophie is playing with the blue teddy *after* she's been taken?"

Alice considered this new bit of information. "Do we speak to Annie Alder again?"

"Too right we do. And this time we want the truth."

Calladine had been listening. "Good work, Ruth. When you see Annie, ask to see the teddy. If she argues the toss, then present her with the evidence."

"Do I tell her we know about the hospital visit?"

"Yes, lay it on. It's about time we got some straight talking from that woman."

"It is possible that someone else took the toy from the house?" Alice suggested. "It might be an idea to get a list of who's visited since that day."

Calladine nodded his agreement. Always one for thoroughness was Alice. "Let me know what happens as soon as."

"Sir!" Joyce called. "Richard Alder is on the line. He sounds angry."

Calladine took the receiver from her.

Alder got straight to the point. "I got another demand. Pay up or they hurt Sophie. Why are you lot still dragging your feet? You should have found her by now. This isn't good enough!"

Calladine's tone was matter-of-fact. "We are working very hard on the case, Mr Alder, I assure you. We are following a number of leads. What have they asked for?"

"The money, what d'you think!" Alder shouted. "I was given account details and told to transfer it immediately. They said they'd contact me later about Sophie. I can't delay for much longer. Heaven knows what they'll do to my child if I do. And I can't reach Annie. I've rung her several times but she isn't answering her mobile."

"Try not to worry," Calladine reassured him. "Annie is still in shock, she might be sleeping. We'll need those bank account details. They are key in tracing the owner of that account."

Calladine gathered the team together for a briefing. "Alder has received a demand for the money from the kidnappers. We're running out of time. We need to clear this one up and quickly." He looked at Rocco and Alice. "You two, see what you can find out about Giles Pennington. I have a suspicion he's not what he seems."

* * *

Frankie Halliwell answered the door to the two detectives. "You lot again. Don't you ever get tired of harassing people?" She'd been drinking and stumbled her way back to the sitting room, where she flopped onto the sofa.

"We'd like to speak to Annie," Ruth said.

"Well, you're out of luck. She's not here and she's not answering my calls either."

"Do you know where she's gone?" Ruth asked.

"No idea. The bitch never tells me anything."

Ruth turned to Alice. "Ring Annie's friend, Joanne. See if she's with her or if she knows where she is."

"We're here to check something," Ruth told Frankie. "Would you fetch Sophie's blue teddy for us please?"

Frankie scowled. "What the hell for? What will that tell you?"

Ruth had to bite back a retort. "Just get it, Frankie, and I'll explain."

Alice had to help the girl to her feet. She reeked of whisky and Alice recoiled.

"I've had a bloody drink! So what!" Frankie shouted at her, almost falling back. "That bloody bloke's really pissed me off. Nothing's ever good enough for him. That stupid sister of mine has a lot to answer for."

Ruth had no idea what she was getting at. "Is your brother-in-law at home?"

"No. He doesn't come home these days if he can help it. Bastard's got a flat at that workplace of his."

"Do you mind if I come with you?" Ruth asked, seeing how unsteady the young woman was. "I don't want you falling on the stairs."

"Do what you like," came the sullen reply.

The child's bedroom was tidy, not a thing out of place. On a shelf was a row of soft toys. The bed, too, was festooned with them. Ruth and Alice both had a good look around, but there was no blue teddy.

Ruth's mobile rang. It was Calladine. She took the call in the hallway.

"How's it going? Is Annie there?"

"No, but her sister, Frankie, is, and she's very drunk. There's no sign of the teddy either."

Ruth heard Calladine sigh. "I don't like this, Ruth. We need to find Annie. I think she is involved in this right up to her neck."

CHAPTER 17

Calladine arrived at Alder's offices with Rocco in tow. The young detective was suspicious about the state of the businessman's finances.

"Trade may be good, but we have to ask where he gets a million from on top of all the investment he's made recently," Rocco voiced as they took the lift up to the top floor.

"That's for another day," Calladine advised. "The man is upset. His daughter is missing. I doubt he's up to an interrogation of his finances right now."

Calladine was right. Alder was genuinely concerned for his daughter's safety. "What's taking you so long?" He banged his fist on the desktop with frustration. "If you lot don't find Sophie soon, I'll have to pay up."

"Calm down, Mr Alder! Paying the ransom isn't the best way to sort this," Calladine said. The detective was well aware that if this was a genuine abduction, then there was nothing to stop whoever had Sophie from hanging onto the child and demanding more money.

"You have the money ready, just in case?" Rocco asked.

"Yes, of course."

Rocco was suspicious. "How did you get your hands on that amount of money so fast, Mr Alder?"

"Why do you need to know that?" Alder asked angrily. "Where the money came from has nothing to do with this. I'm just glad I have it to pay over if needs be."

Calladine saw Alder's eyes narrow. The man was hiding something. "We need to move quickly." He addressed Alder. "Give me a copy of the email with the transfer details and I'll get our experts working on it."

"I've printed you a copy."

The bank account details were standard enough. "This is a UK account," Calladine told them. "In the name of Jones."

"Very original," Alder scoffed.

"Do you know where your wife is, sir?" Calladine asked.

There was silence. The question was unexpected. "Have you tried her friend, Joanne?" His voice was suddenly calm. "Annie confides in her, tells her more these days than she tells me."

"Do you have her number?"

Alder tapped the number into his mobile phone and passed it over. "Joanne? This is DI Calladine. Is Annie with you?" Short and simple. Minutes later, the call was over. "Joanne hasn't seen her since yesterday. She hasn't spoken to her on the phone either."

Calladine went out into the corridor and rang Ruth, who was still at the Alder's house. "Find out if Annie has taken anything with her."

"You think she's done one?"

"If Annie has anything to do with this, she'll have left. The ransom is to be paid by bank transfer into a UK account at the abductor's request. We're not dealing with experienced criminals here."

"Easily traceable in that case."

"That's what I'm thinking. The account is in the name of Jones. Find out if the account holder ever visited the bank in person. If so, get the CCTV. We need to move fast, and we need to find Annie. She holds the key to this."

"Give me a moment, I'll have a look in her room." Ruth kept the line open as she started her search.

Frankie Halliwell was sleeping off the drink in one of the bedrooms, so Ruth had the run of the house. She walked across the landing to the master bedroom. Women's clothes were strewn across the bed. "I think she's gone," she told Calladine, who was waiting on the phone. "From the state of the bedroom, I'd say she's packed a bag and left." Ruth checked the dressing table. "All her cosmetics and jewellery have gone too. This looks like the work of a woman in a hurry."

"Thanks, Ruth." He hung up.

Rocco had followed Calladine out into the corridor. "Any chance of getting a warrant to look at the Alder accounts?"

"What do you suspect him of?"

"I'm not sure, but the figures don't add up."

"Rocco, you don't know that for sure. You haven't seen the figures. We have no idea how much the factory makes. Anyway, we've got more urgent matters to attend to. If it becomes vital to the investigation, then I will ask for a warrant. But until then we can only look at what Alder allows us to."

"The new factory and office buildings alone must have cost a fortune, not to mention that house of theirs. And now the ransom money. He's told us he has the cash ready. That amount came from somewhere," Rocco pushed.

Calladine shook his head and went back into Alder's office. "Your wife is missing, sir. She's packed some of her stuff and disappeared."

"What are you're telling me?"

"I'm not sure myself, yet. But it is possible that Annie is somehow connected with Sophie's disappearance."

Alder frowned. "I don't understand. Why would she do that?"

"I've no idea. But if she gets in touch, let me know immediately."

"I know your new chief superintendent, Calladine. We'll see what he has to say about this. He'll make bringing my wife and daughter home a priority."

Calladine ignored the threat and left him to it. They needed to get back and speak to the techies. He tossed Rocco his car keys. "What are you thinking?"

Rocco looked thoughtful. "I'm puzzled, that's all. Have you considered that Richard Alder might have something else going on apart from manufacturing biscuits?"

"Do you have any suggestions?"

"No. But I'm not happy."

* * *

Calladine needed to know if Annie was behind the abduction of her daughter. Only then would he be satisfied that Sophie Alder was not in any immediate danger. But the bank confirmed that Wendy Jones had only been to the branch once to open the account and that was several months ago. There was no CCTV available.

"What d'you reckon?" Rocco asked Calladine. "Is Annie Alder behind this?"

"At the moment I've got an open mind." He watched Rocco yawn. It had been a long day. "I'll wait and see what comes through. You get off."

"I won't say no, if you're sure?"

"See you in the morning," Calladine said.

He made himself a strong coffee and settled down to read through the Sean Barber murder file one more time. It might be a long wait.

CHAPTER 18

Ruth went straight home after visiting the Alder house. Calladine was happy to wait for any results and there was nothing she could do. But on entering the house, Ruth wished she had somewhere else to be. Harry was screaming his lungs out and there was a strong smell of burning coming from the kitchen.

"Ruined the chicken, I'm afraid." Jake gave her a sheepish smile. "I can't get the hang of the new oven. And it's been bedlam round here tonight. I think there's some sort of rave going on at the top end of the close. I haven't checked because I didn't want to take Harry outside in the cold, but they've been chucking fireworks about and music is blaring out of the end house."

Ruth frowned. "Old Mr Hopkins lives there. That doesn't sound like him. Has he got visitors?"

"A black Range Rover went roaring up a couple of hours ago, and there's been a steady stream of vehicles since. If there'd been kids playing, they wouldn't have stood a chance."

"I'll go and have a word, make sure he's okay." Ruth surveyed the kitchen. How could one man and a child make so much mess! Jake was usually fine with the cooking.

"There's a casserole in the freezer. Whack it in the microwave. I won't be long."

Ruth put her coat back on and walked the few metres to the elderly man's house.

Jake was right. Mr Hopkins' house was lit up like a beacon and the front door was wide open — no need to knock then. Ruth could hear voices and music. A tall, dark-haired lad stood in the kitchen doorway, handing out cans of beer.

"What's going on?" she demanded. "Where is Mr Hopkins?"

The lad spun round and grinned at her. "Nosy old bat!" he said. "We put him to bed. He were tired, couldn't keep up."

"Who are you?" She had to raise her voice over the blaring music.

He sniggered. "I'm his grandson, David."

"And this lot?"

"Me mates. It's cool, no need to stress. Me grandad don't mind."

"We'll see about that." Ruth climbed the staircase. "Mr Hopkins, you okay?" She tried the bedroom door but it was locked from the inside. "It's Ruth, from down the close. Will you come out?"

A few seconds later she heard the key turn in the lock. "They're off their heads. Wrecking the place." The elderly man was obviously anxious. "Please get rid of them. I've tried, but all they do is laugh at me."

"Is that lad David your grandson?"

Mr Hopkins shook his head. "Is he heck. I don't know him from Adam, and he's not called David either. They turned up here uninvited. I can't do anything. There's too many of them and they're a right rough lot."

Ruth had heard enough. "Don't worry, Mr Hopkins. I'll sort them out."

Ruth was pissed off. Back downstairs she went straight to the radio and turned it off. A collective groan went round the room. "Want to spend the night in the nick?" she asked, holding up her warrant card.

"Got some front, that one." A comment from one of the group. "She needs teaching a lesson."

Ruth looked round at them. There was a mix of lads and girls. What did they think they were doing? Some were lying on the carpet, obviously out of it. Others were lolling on the furniture. There were no lights on, but she could still see sleeping bags, duvets and clothing littered about. There was dirty crockery and what appeared to be dust covering every surface. This wasn't new. This lot had been here a while.

"Get out and don't come back, or that's what will happen." She looked at the scowling faces. She recognised one of them. "I know you, Dean Laycock. I'll be speaking to your parents in the morning." It flashed through Ruth's mind that the lad had changed a lot since she'd last seen him. He'd lost weight for a start and looked positively haggard.

Another of the lads laughed and pushed Dean forward towards Ruth while whispering something in his ear. "Come on lads. The tart wants us gone. Time we moved on. This is a boring old hole anyway."

Ruth saw him nod at Dean, then the lad bent down and picked up a large holdall. "Drop that!" she shouted.

"No way!"

"I won't ask again."

She heard some of the group snigger. The bag was obviously important. The lad clutched it close to his body. "Drop it or I'll arrest you."

"Do her now, Dean," the call went up.

Dean walked towards her. He had one hand in his pocket. The lad with the holdall had gone.

Dean looked unsteady on his feet and stumbled as he moved toward Ruth. "He warned you," he hissed under his breath. "You should have let it go. You can't take this lot on, you won't win."

"Last chance," she warned. "I know you and you're in big trouble. I want names and I want that holdall."

Ruth heard the others muttering. One shouted, "Go on, do her now!"

Suddenly Dean lunged at her. She saw the glint of a blade. He'd been holding a knife in his pocket. She should have realised. But Ruth reacted quickly, lifting her arm so her hand was protecting her body, but the blade still caught her. She stumbled back in shock and fell, hitting her head on the stone hearth of the fireplace. The blow knocked her out cold.

* * *

Ruth came round to bright lights and the sound of voices. Her head hurt like hell and her right hand was heavily bandaged. She'd no idea what had happened, but it had to be serious — she was in hospital.

"Ruth, can you hear me?"

It was Jake. He looked concerned. "Where am I?" she asked softly. Her mouth was so dry she could barely speak. "Where's Harry?"

"He's fine. The neighbour is sitting with him. You were attacked. You went to see Mr Hopkins, remember?"

Ruth closed her eyes. She was sleepy. She had a vague recollection of seeing a group of youngsters, an angry rabble. They'd frightened Mr Hopkins and she'd tackled them.

A doctor spoke. "She hasn't come round properly yet. She'll be more coherent tomorrow."

Ruth could hear the words but they made no sense. Something was nudging at the edge of her memory. It was frustrating. She had to tell them something, but what? Her eyes snapped open and she looked at the people around her. She only recognised Jake. No Calladine. She needed to speak to him urgently, but Ruth couldn't remember why.

"Calladine?" she whispered to Jake.

"Don't stress, I'll ring him later. You have to rest. Work can wait."

"Mr Hopkins?"

"He's fine. I rang his doctor. He'll get sorted, don't worry."

But Ruth *was* worried. Something was seriously wrong. The detail kept slipping out of reach. She groaned in pain. Jake was right, it would have to wait.

CHAPTER 19

Day 4

Calladine had stayed late in the incident room waiting for forensic results to come in from either the Sean Barber killing or the Alder abduction. Neither had been forthcoming so he'd called it a day. On arriving at the station the next morning, he was greeted by an anxious desk sergeant.

"Have you heard about Ruth, sir?" The officer looked worried. Something was wrong. But surely if something serious had happened to Ruth then Jake would have called him.

Calladine frowned. "What about her?"

"She's in hospital. Some sort of ruck on her street. A bunch of kids got rough and she was stabbed."

Calladine's stomach turned over. He immediately made his way back out to the car park. What the hell was going on? Why hadn't anyone told him? If anything happened to Ruth, well, he'd no idea what he'd do. His seriously doubted his ability to carry on in the job.

He hadn't asked, but Calladine presumed that Ruth would be in the infirmary. He drove straight there.

Running up the main corridor, he saw Doc Hoyle coming out of his office.

"She's fine," the doc said at once. "Good God man, you need to calm down. You're as white as a sheet."

Calladine was out of breath from running. "Is it any wonder? What the hell happened? Can I see her?"

"Ruth's okay. I've just come from giving her the all-clear. She's waiting for a taxi to take her home."

"A taxi! Where's Jake, why isn't he with her? What's going on in that bloke's head?"

"She's in the side room at the end. Go and speak to her yourself."

Calladine was furious. Ruth shouldn't be on her own. Jake should've taken the day off. She'd need looking after.

As he entered the room Ruth looked up and smiled at him. She was dressed and sat on the bed, an overnight bag at her side.

"Christ, you look worse than me!" she said. "Give you a fright, did I?"

"I'd no idea how serious your injuries were. I was just told that you'd been stabbed. How d'you imagine I felt?"

"Well, I'm fine." She waved a bandaged hand at him. "It looks worse than it is. You know what it's like, more bandage than wound."

Calladine nodded at the overnight bag. "No need for a taxi, I'll take you," he said. "I'm surprised Jake has left you here like this."

Ruth rolled her eyes. "He's got work and Harry to see to. We're not the only ones with demanding jobs, you know. Anyway, I insisted that I could see to myself."

Calladine wasn't convinced. She'd banged her head, probably had concussion. Plus, her hand was heavily bandaged. They didn't do that for a scratch. "How did this happen? It's usually so quiet where you live."

"Not recently, from all accounts. I've been so busy, I've not noticed. Old Mr Hopkins at the end of Orchard Close has had a group of youngsters staying with him, and not out of choice. They're a rough bunch. One of them said he was his grandson, but a load of rubbish."

"I don't understand. Are these kids homeless or something? How did it happen? Did they just turn up and move in?"

"Sort of. And they'd been there a while from the look of things. There were sleeping bags and clothes lying around. A lot of rubbish, cans and takeaway trays." Ruth paused. "I challenged them because of the noise. They were playing loud music and cars had been roaring up and down day and night. They didn't like my interference, but I had to try and stop them. Did no good though, not even my warrant card bothered them. One of them, Dean Laycock, went for me with a blade. If I hadn't dodged it, stuck up my hand in defence, he might've killed me. Uniform are bringing him in. Mind you, he was being egged on by the others. He lunged for me, I moved, but when I felt the blade, I tripped and banged my head on the hearth. I was unconscious for a while. Fortunately, Mr Hopkins had left the house and was already on his way back with Jake. Some of the other neighbours came out, too. I presume when the group saw what they were up against, they legged it. That house needs forensics round pronto."

"Why didn't Mr Hopkins just call the police to begin with?"

"He has no mobile, only a landline. The kids must have broken it. Besides, he's an old man and he was frightened. I expect they threatened him."

Calladine frowned. "What were these kids doing?"

"Can't you guess? Think about it. Mr Hopkins, Rowena Hargreaves, and Alex Geddes. What do they all have in common, Tom?"

Calladine scratched his head. "Two of them are pensioners, but Alex was a young lad."

"They are all vulnerable people, easily manipulated," Ruth explained. "They were targeted by this group. They seek out a likely candidate, move in, get them hooked on dope and take over."

"Then what? What is it they want?"

"One of the lads, I've never seen him before, had a large holdall. I told him to drop it, but he refused. Clung onto it like grim death. It was at that point that things got dodgy." She looked at Calladine. He still hadn't got it. "Have you heard the term 'cuckooing?'"

Calladine was baffled. "I think there was a mention in that circular we got. I glimpsed it, but you know how it is."

"Well, I've read about it. A group move in with a vulnerable person, usually only one or two for starters. For a while they appear kind. Do the shopping, a little cooking. But that soon changes. The rest of the group arrive and they take over. They use the premises as a drugs den. All deliveries and pick-ups, and a lot of using, is done from that address. They constantly move around, which means they stay one step ahead of us."

"You worked all this out while you lay injured in here?"

Ruth smiled. "Nothing else to do, is there? Battery's dead on my mobile."

"Rocco had noticed how quiet the streets are. All uniform has stopped is the odd possession. There's been no dealing that we're aware of."

"Oh, it's going on alright, but under wraps."

At that moment Calladine's mobile rang. It was Alice. He listened intently to what she told him.

"DNA's in on the blood found on those wood splinters," he told Ruth at the end of the call.

"I've been thinking about that case, too." Ruth smiled knowingly.

"The blood belongs to Annie Alder. It looks like we've all been set up," Calladine told her.

Ruth stood up gingerly. "You need to get back to the station. But you can drop me home on the way. I'll spend the rest of the day with my feet up and see you tomorrow. Make sure forensics get to Mr Hopkins' house today."

"There's no need to rush back. With an injured hand, you won't be able to drive."

"That's not all I do, you know." Ruth laughed. "Anyway, you're pushed, you need me. A day tops, and then it's work as normal."

CHAPTER 20

A relieved Calladine made his way back to the station. Ruth was okay, but that was more down to luck than anything else. Dean Laycock would be charged. Attempted murder. The lad would also be questioned about the mysterious 'Street.' Sooner or later, either he or one of his group would talk.

There was also the question of Annie Alder. It was her blood they'd found on the wood splinters. Their instincts had been right all along. But what Calladine couldn't understand was why she hadn't simply left Alder, without all the drama. He decided to speak to her sister, Frankie, see what she could tell them.

"Dean Laycock, has he been arrested?" he asked as he entered the office.

Alice looked up from her desk. "He's downstairs in the cells, sir. He's asked for a solicitor. The one he specified has been contacted. Not the duty one either. This solicitor is from some large practice in Oldston."

"There's money in dealing drugs. Do we know if it's drug money he's using to pay?"

"He won't say, sir. He simply gave us the number to ring."

Calladine nodded. "I'll deal with him later. I want a word with Frankie Halliwell, but first I must speak to Richard Alder.

"Have you found her?" His first words when he heard Calladine's voice.

"We're getting there. It's important that you don't pay the ransom over," he said. "We have evidence that your wife may be implicated in the abduction."

There was silence on the line. Calladine understood that this would be confusing for Alder.

"Annie took Sophie! Are you sure?" He said at last.

"We've got evidence that points that way. When we do find your wife and child, you will be the first to know, in the meantime, do not transfer any money."

Reluctantly, Alder agreed.

"Alice, you're with me."

He waited for DC Bolshaw to grab her jacket and then the pair headed for the car park.

"How's Ruth?" Alice asked, once they were outside.

"She reckons she's fine, but then that's Ruth all over, isn't it? It was a near miss from all accounts. That hooligan, Laycock, will get his, don't worry."

Alice looked relieved. "You think Annie Alder faked the kidnapping?"

"Yes, I do. But what I can't work out is why."

"Perhaps she was afraid of her husband?" Alice suggested.

"Possibly. I will find out and get an explanation. This investigation has cost both time and money."

Once again Frankie Halliwell answered the door to the Alder house. She was pale and heavy eyed, nursing a hangover. She greeted the pair with a grimace. Calladine noticed the suitcases in the hall.

"Going somewhere?" he asked.

"Yes. Not that it's got anything to do with you."

"We might need to get in touch. A forwarding address would be useful."

Frankie scowled at him. "I'll be at my place on the Hobfield."

Calladine glanced behind her into the house. "Is Annie in?"

"She's done one. Said nowt, just packed and went. I hate her! She had everything, but the cow still went and stole the only man I ever had a chance with."

The bitterness Frankie felt towards her sister was evident. Her face was red now and there were tears of frustration on her cheeks.

"Where's she gone, Frankie?" Alice asked gently.

"Off with Billy, Rick's older brother. Damn sod promised me we'd be together. Didn't mean a word of it, lying bastard. She bats her eyelashes and he's smitten. Stupid lump! I hate him too!"

Calladine was puzzled. "Is this relationship new?"

"No. The pair of them have been working on their plan to scam Rick for a while. All that time Billy strung me along to cover their tracks. He kept telling me that we had a future. Wish I'd never set eyes on him."

"We need to find Annie. Do you know where they might have gone?" Calladine asked.

"No. I can't find either of them. But when I do, they'll be sorry they crossed me. That man doesn't know what's coming to him."

"You shouldn't make threats, Frankie," Calladine said.

The young woman looked angry. "I'm not making threats, I mean every word. I'll get my own back. The pair of them will be sorry they did this to me."

"You didn't know about the affair?" Alice asked.

"I suspected Annie had someone. But I never for one second thought it was Billy. I hate him! I hate them both!" She looked at Calladine. "This whole thing was a set-up. Telling you lot the kid had been taken, everything. She did it to get money out of Rick, but she won't get away with it." Frankie shook her mobile phone at them. "I've told her exactly what I'm going to do. Rick doesn't know yet what she's done. He doesn't know about Billy either. I'm going to tell him. Then we'll see. Rick will find them and they'll get paid back. Annie will regret what she did to me, and Billy will wish he'd never set eyes on the bitch."

"You've spoken to Annie?" Calladine asked.

Frankie looked at him. "She's not picking up, so I texted. She will be one scared woman when she reads it, believe me. Richard Alder is not a man you mess with, he's got too much to lose." Frankie folded her arms. "Why are you asking me all these questions? What have you found out?"

"Not a lot and that's the problem. What I don't understand is why Annie went to all that trouble. If she wanted out, why not just tell Richard it was over, leave and take Sophie with her."

"Because Rick is a control freak, that's why. No way would he let her take Sophie, or give her money."

"He seems the reasonable sort to me," Calladine said.

"Well he's not. Far from it. All that big-hearted businessman stuff is a sham. Richard Alder is nothing but a well-dressed thug. Annie wanted out almost as soon as she'd married him. Silly bitch realised too late as usual. You should have heard her, she told me all about the things he did. What a heavy-handed bully he was."

"Are you sure you don't know where Annie's gone?" Calladine asked again.

"No idea. But she'd better not show herself until things calm down."

At least it had cleared up one puzzle. Annie's new boyfriend, Billy Alder, was Sophie's uncle. That's why she hadn't been afraid to go with him, but little Jack simply knew him as the man in a witch costume at the party.

* * *

Calladine and Alice headed back to the station. "We should pay a visit to Alf Alder's place," Calladine declared. "Billy lived with him. It's possible there's a computer or something that'll give us a clue as to where Annie and him have gone."

Alice was driving. "Shouldn't we speak to the young villain who attacked Ruth, sir? We need to know a lot more about that group he was with and this person 'Street,' who leads them."

Calladine wanted that too. But the Alder case was bugging him. He intended to have a word with the CPS, find out what they could charge Annie Alder with, if anything. Sophie was her child, so not abduction. Apart from wasting police time, he couldn't come up with anything. But it had been an elaborate plan — why was that necessary? What was she was running from?

"A quick stop off at Heron House and then back to the nick to sort out that hooligan. Don't worry," he told Alice, "Dean Laycock isn't going anywhere."

* * *

Alf Alder lived on the second floor of Heron House, one of the tower blocks on the Hobfield estate. He was a man old before his time. He'd been a smoker since his teens and coughed between each sentence he spoke.

"I haven't seen him for a day or two. Buggered off, he has. Taken that lass with him. Stupid fool. Our Rick'll have him for dinner!" Alf said.

"Did Billy have a computer, or a mobile phone that he might have left behind?" Calladine asked.

Alf shrugged. "He had an old one. Kept it in his room. Billy never bothered much with computers. As for a mobile, I suppose he must have, but he never rang me."

They'd gone somewhere, Billy, Annie and Sophie, and that took planning. "Did he talk about going away lately, perhaps on a holiday?" Alice suggested.

"Not that I remember. Kept his thoughts to himself, did Billy. If you find him, tell him to get home. Them kids drive me mad most nights and that's his fault too."

"Why's that, Alf?" Calladine asked.

"Dunno. Summat do with footie I suppose. But they're a rough set of little buggers. Scare me half to death."

"How did Billy get on with his brother?"

"Hated our Rick. Didn't much like the way he lorded it over him. When Rick gave him that garage job, it were final straw. The two had a big bust up. Our Rick saw'th light. He gave Billy the title of transport manager, not that he had any experience. It were just to keep peace." The man coughed again. "Don't know what he expected. He's got no qualifications, our Billy, just good with engines. He's damn lucky to have Rick to crawl to."

Calladine had a quick look round the small flat. Billy's room was tidy. There wasn't much, just a bed, empty wardrobe and chest of drawers with a few clothes still in it. He picked up the laptop from the bedside table. Billy's wallet was lying on it too. It didn't look like Billy Alder had gone very far.

"Sir," Alice called. "What d'you reckon to this lot?"

She was holding a pile of newspapers.

"They're fairly recent but not local. Several are Welsh papers. It would seem that Billy was looking at property there. You can see from the pages he's left them open at."

"I doubt they're important, but bring them along just in case." Calladine turned to Alf. "Okay if we take them?"

"Help yourself. Save me taking them down to'th recycling bin."

"We've got Billy's laptop too. If he comes back, let us know at once will you?" Alf was sitting in an armchair by the fire. He looked frail. "Here, take this." Calladine handed him his card. "It's got my direct line on it. Any trouble, give us a ring."

CHAPTER 21

Back at the station, Calladine decided he and Rocco would interview Dean Laycock.

"How old is he?" he asked Rocco as they walked down the corridor to the interview room.

"He's eighteen, so old enough, and his solicitor is with him. Odd that. The guy is expensive. I can't see Laycock or his family affording him."

"Drug money? Or something more sinister?"

Rocco looked at him. "What d'you mean, guv?"

"That there's someone behind all this pulling the strings. The individual known as 'Street,' for example."

"If he exists. We can't find any trace of him."

"Oh, he exists alright. I can feel it in my gut. Besides, as Alice told us, the kids know him."

The two detectives sat down opposite Dean and his solicitor. James Delaney was from a large practice in Oldston. He did not look impressed and had put several feet between him and Laycock. Not his usual bill of fare? That begged the question, who had hired him?

"Tell me what happened last night at Mr Hopkins' house on Orchard Close," Calladine began.

"No comment," came the smug reply.

Laycock tapped his fingers impatiently on the table. He was jittery. If this was about drugs, perhaps the lad needed a fix. This was par for the course for the detectives, but Calladine could see that Laycock was irritating the solicitor.

"You had some friends round, had the music playing loud, and opened a few cans. That's right, isn't it?"

An unflinching stare followed by another, "No comment."

Calladine sighed. The lad was playing the hard man. "Okay, Dean, have it your way. At this rate we'll be here all night and I've got better things to do." He turned to the solicitor. But Delaney merely shrugged.

"I'm being well paid for my services. I'm in no hurry." He smiled.

Calladine turned his attention back to Laycock. "You attacked one of my officers. You deliberately went for her with a blade. She was injured, she could've been killed." Calladine paused to give the lad a chance to say his piece. Nothing. "You won't talk to me, so I won't waste my time. You will be charged with attempted murder."

"You can't keep me here!" Laycock barked back. "I need to get out."

"Getting twitchy, Dean? Last dose of whatever rubbish you're taking wearing off, is it? Well, hard luck."

"Bail?" Delaney asked.

"Refused. Your client is a dangerous young man. Time spent in the cells will give him the opportunity to think." He looked at the lad. "I want to know about last night. I also want to know about the individual known as 'Street.' Cooperate and things might go easier for you."

"Charge him," he said to Rocco as he walked through the door.

Back in the incident room, Calladine studied the board. "Do we have an update on the PM on Sean Barber?"

"Apparently the Duggan has been busy. Not a nice thought." Alice shuddered. "Dr Barrington left a message. She wants you to ring her."

Calladine picked up the phone. He was curious about what sort of blade had killed Barber.

"It was long and narrow," Natasha confirmed. "I suspected you'd be curious, want to know if it was similar to the one that Ruth was attacked with. I visited her in the infirmary. The blade Ruth was slashed with had a serrated edge. A kitchen knife, for example. The killer's blade was more of a stiletto." He knew these knives — they had long, slender blades with a needle-like point.

"Not a match then. I suppose that's something. We're going with the Barber killing being down to vigilantes. Ruth's attack was something else."

"I have already started the PM on Sean Barber. He's covered in bruises, as you'd expect from someone who was beaten up. He also has a fractured skull. But apart from that and the knife wound, there's not a lot else. I'll send the report through to you when I'm finished. Save you a trip here."

"Okay, thanks, but if you do find anything else, let me know immediately, will you? Also, once you've finished, will you release the body? I know his mother and she'll be anxious to sort the funeral."

"No problem, Tom. Forensics are scouring Mr Hopkins' house on Orchard Close. They've found white powder all over the place, we're presuming its cocaine, although we've only tested a small sample. If the rest turns out to be cocaine, then there must have been a fortune in drugs in that house. I'm at a loss to understand what's going on. They're kids. Where on earth are they getting it from?"

That was exactly what Calladine wanted to know. "We're working on the assumption that the house was being used as a temporary drugs den. The same with the flat belonging to Alex Geddes and an elderly woman called Rowena Hargreaves. The group moves in and takes the place over."

Natasha sounded thoughtful. "I've read about that. If what you say is right then you're looking for whoever is organising the group or groups at the top."

"All we have is a nickname — 'Street.' Ring any bells with you?"

He heard Natasha laugh. "No, sorry. Not my scene, I'm afraid."

"DI Calladine, a word in my office."

It was DCI Birch. She was standing at the doorway and she did not look happy. Calladine ended the call to Natasha and followed her down the corridor, wondering what he'd done now.

"I've had DCS Chesworth on the phone again. He wants this mess sorting and quick."

"We're doing our best, ma'am. We now believe that the child abduction was a scam instigated by the mother. She's run off with Billy Alder. We may need to find them."

"Chesworth wants you to drop it."

"Suits me. The Barber killing has to take priority. The Alder case is a waste of our time. The child is hers, therefore no abduction. Case closed."

Birch nodded her approval. "Good. No more chasing shadows. Shame we've been side-tracked. Sean Barber's killer has had time to make good his escape."

"We don't have much on that one, ma'am. But we know it's linked to the drug dealing. On that front, we have to find the individual known as 'Street.'"

He saw Birch stiffen. "Chesworth says no on that one. He does not want him apprehending."

"With due respect, ma'am, I don't think Chesworth has a clue what we're up against. Apart from Barber, we've got the attack on DS Bayliss and a group of drug-dealing kids to deal with. We're working flat out as it." He thought for a moment. "What's Chesworth's interest in Street, ma'am?"

She looked grim. "I've no idea. Use uniform and get Thorpe to pull his weight. That should lessen the load a little."

Calladine didn't understand. "This 'Street' is key to several of our enquiries, ma'am. I need to bring him in."

Birch sat down behind her desk. "Do as you're told, Calladine," she said sharply. "Forget about this 'Street.' Instead, concentrate on finding Barber's killer."

Calladine stared at her. "We can't simply ignore the information we have about 'Street.' For all we know, it could be him who murdered Barber. We also believe he's behind the distribution of drugs locally."

She looked at him stonily. "I will not tell you again. Forget him."

He knew he was chancing his luck. Birch was in no mood for an interrogation. "Is 'Street' an informant? Is that why you want him left alone?"

"This conversation is over." Birch pointed to her office door.

Calladine had no idea what to make of all this. He returned to the incident room. He was curious about Birch's directive regarding 'Street.' Originally, that had come from Chesworth. Why was the new DCS getting involved?

"Natasha Barrington tells me that the house on Ruth's close has cocaine residue all through it," he told the team. "Those kids had to have been using it to both receive, cut and distribute drugs. We need to know who is behind that. Dean Laycock certainly hasn't got the brains." He turned to Rocco. "Did you get his phone when he was arrested?"

"Yes, guv," Rocco replied. "We're getting the data from his provider."

Calladine nodded at him. "We could do with that quickly."

"There's been no whispers, apart from the name 'Street' being bandied about," Rocco told the team. "Like I said, all's quiet on the drugs front currently."

"Someone is behind this. It might be this 'Street,' it might be someone else. We should ask ourselves where the stuff is coming from."

"Some big-time dealer?" Alice suggested.

"Possibly, but who is he? I suspect those kids have been doing this for a while. That means they've shifted a load of cocaine in the last few months. Someone has turned over a fortune."

"By the way, sir, Rowena Hargreaves has identified a number of items in the haul recovered from Sean Barber's bedroom," Alice said. "Apparently she's well pleased."

That was good news. At least someone was happy. Calladine's mobile rang. It was Zoe.

"Come for tea tonight," she invited. "Jo thinks we should talk some more about the baby. There's things you should know."

That piqued Calladine's curiosity. She was pregnant, and he was pleased, so what else was there to say?

"You don't have to worry about me, Zo. I'm fine about the baby. You'll make a great mum."

"It's not as simple as that, Dad. Come about five, and don't be late."

CHAPTER 22

Zoe had gone to a great deal of trouble. She'd set the table in the dining room and Calladine could smell roast beef.

"Thought I'd make it special. Now that Layla's gone, I bet you're not eating much." She pointed him towards the sitting room. "Get yourself a glass of wine. Jo's in there with our other guest."

Calladine was curious. Who else was invited? He'd thought this was a family gathering to discuss the baby. He was doubly confused when he saw the other guest was Julian Batho. What was he doing here?

"Good to see you, Julian," he greeted the professor. "You're looking a lot chipper than you did the other day."

Julian was chatting with Jo and had a smile on his face. A rare event — something had cheered him up.

"This pair told you their news?" Calladine asked.

Julian gave him an odd look. "You don't know, do you?"

Jo returned with Zoe in tow. "Before we all start talking at cross-purposes, we'd better explain," she smiled. Zoe cleared her throat. "Julian is part of this too, dad," she said. "He's the baby's father."

Calladine was momentarily shocked. He'd realised that there must be a father, a donor, but had thought it would be someone anonymous, found by the fertility clinic. So how had this pair persuaded Julian? And more to the point, how had this been achieved?

"I can see the cogs turning." Zoe laughed. "Everything was carried out at the clinic, and done properly. Except that we took our own donor along. The arrangement suits us all, so you can take that frown off your face."

Calladine hadn't realised he was frowning. He was pleased for Zoe, but Julian as the child's father? That was something else. "I'm just a bit taken aback, that's all," he said, and stepped forward to shake Julian's hand. "This is totally unexpected. I'd no idea you wanted children."

"I hadn't thought about it until I spoke to Zoe," Julian admitted. "She asked me to recommend a clinic. After what happened to Imogen, I need something, someone, in my life. I'm struggling, if I'm honest. I have a huge hole to fill. I don't want someone new, not yet. But this is no hasty decision. I thought long and hard, and for me it seems the perfect solution. The three of us will parent the child together. He or she will know me as its dad."

Calladine had his doubts. "You're a workaholic, Julian. And I don't mean anything by this, but what do you know about raising kids?"

"No more or less than anyone else, Tom. But you have to appreciate that this is a done deal. The baby is a reality. In a few months he or she will be part of this family."

In that instant Calladine realised that Julian would be part of his family too, whether he liked it or not. "Have you told your aunt?" Amy Dean and her sister were the only family Julian had.

"Amy is fine about it. She's planning to visit quite soon, so you can ask her yourself."

Calladine's stomach lurched. He and Amy had once been an item. He'd not known at first that she was related to Julian. Amy, or Amaris, her professional name, had run a 'new age' shop in Leesdon. He'd asked for her help while investigating what he'd called the 'tarot card' murders.

"The food's ready," Zoe announced. She handed Julian a bottle of red wine and smiled. "I can't, but the rest of you enjoy."

Calladine watched Julian follow Jo into the kitchen for a corkscrew. The three of them seemed happy and relaxed in each other's company. If this worked, if Julian accepted the responsibility without going overboard, it would do him the world of good.

* * *

Calladine arrived home later than he'd expected. Despite his earlier reservations, it had been an enjoyable evening. Zoe, Jo and Julian had chatted happily about the impending new arrival. Odd as it was, he'd actually felt like a gooseberry.

He was ready to turn in. A quick walk around the block with Sam and he'd call it a day. He'd been home no more than five minutes when there was a knock on his front door. It was Kat Barber.

"They're releasing my Sean at the end of the week," she said. "I can lay him to rest now."

"You'll feel better when it's over," he reassured her.

Kat smiled at him. "I know it was down to you. Thank you. You've been a great help and I won't forget it."

Calladine was about to ask her in when his mobile rang. With Kat still standing at the door he answered it. It was Rocco.

"There's been another stabbing, sir," Rocco said. "On the lane that runs along the back of the Hobfield, the one that backs onto the rough ground. Sir . . ." he paused.

"What is it, Rocco?"

"I'm down there now. The victim's dead — it's Frankie Halliwell."

Calladine was stunned. He was tired and didn't want to drag himself to the scene, but he had no choice. He ended the call and turned back to Kat.

"I'm sorry, Kat. I'd invite you in, but something's happened and I have to go out. I don't know when I'll be back."

She nodded understandingly. "Come for a meal tomorrow evening, when you've finished work. I'll cook us something nice." She reached up and kissed him on the cheek.

* * *

Calladine arrived at the scene to find Natasha Barrington and the CSI team hard at it.

"She's had a right going over. There are bruises on her face and torso," the pathologist said.

"Did she try to fight back? Is there anything under her nails?"

"Unlikely. They're bitten to the quick."

"Pity. Is her stuff still here, her mobile?"

"You think it was a robbery, sir?" Rocco asked, coming forward. "More like Billy Alder getting even. Frankie threatened to tell his brother, don't forget. That gives him a pretty good motive for murder."

That seemed a little too simple to Calladine. They didn't even know if Billy and Annie were still in the area. "We'll reserve judgement for now," Calladine replied. "Is her stuff still here?" he repeated.

"No. There's nothing, not even in her pockets," Natasha confirmed. "I can't be sure until I get her back, but this wound looks very like the one inflicted on Sean Barber. Narrow and deep, the type a stiletto blade would make."

That was not what Calladine was expecting. If Natasha was right, then the two murders were linked. But how could that be? They were different cases. Sean Barber had been a member of the cuckooing group, but Frankie Halliwell hadn't.

Calladine took charge. "Seal off this area for now. Let's make sure we bag every bit of evidence there is." He looked at Natasha. "When will you do this one?"

"Tomorrow morning."

"I'll see you at nine," he replied.

CHAPTER 23

Day 5

Ruth was in the office bright and early the next morning, but Calladine was nowhere to be seen. "Where is he?" she asked Thorpe, who was sitting at the spare desk tucking into a bacon barm. "And where's Rocco? Here's me making a supreme effort while the rest bunk off."

"Frankie Halliwell was murdered last night," Thorpe told her, his mouth full. "Stabbed she was. The boss has gone to the Duggan."

He said the words as if it was nothing at all, but Ruth was shocked. "Who'd want to kill Frankie?"

"I reckon it's down to Billy Alder. He and Annie tried to scam the ransom out of Richard and have gone into hiding. Frankie threatened them. From what I've heard about Billy, he wouldn't like that."

Ruth thought it wasn't the worst explanation "Are we absolutely sure the scam was down to Annie?"

"Your mate, Rocco, will soon find out. The CCTV's in from the bank in Oldston."

That was something at least. "Did Calladine say when he'd be back?"

Thorpe shrugged. "No idea."

Typical Thorpe, Ruth thought. The sooner Long came back and took him off their hands, the better.

"Do we have any idea yet where Annie and Billy have gone," Ruth asked them.

"Alice and the boss went to Alf Alder's flat yesterday," Rocco said. "They brought back Billy's laptop and that pile of newspapers." He gestured at a filing cabinet. "Looks like Billy's been looking for a place to hide over the last few weeks. Not all of those papers are local. Alice thought they might prove useful."

"Is the laptop being looked at?" Ruth asked.

Rocco nodded a reply.

"We'd better start looking through these then," Ruth said, handing a few papers to each of them. "Billy bought this little lot for a reason. I bet you're right, he was looking for a bolthole for him and Annie. A long way away from the look of some of these."

"This one's the *Mid-Wales Gazette*," Rocco said.

"Makes sense. They don't want to bump into Richard, do they?"

* * *

Frankie Halliwell had been beaten and stabbed. There were multiple bruises on her body.

As agreed, Calladine had arrived at the Duggan Centre early that morning. Natasha had Frankie laid out on the slab and had completed the post-mortem examination. "There was a lot of blood on her clothes and she was missing a trainer, but it was found and forensics have it," she said. "It was discovered some distance away. It's possible that she took it off and threw it at whoever was after her."

"Didn't help much, did it?" Calladine commented. "Poor lass is a mess."

"You're right there. She's had a right going-over." Natasha paused, her mouth a thin line. "The stab wound is to her chest. Your killer knew what he was doing. There'll have to be tests, of course, but I'm pretty certain it's the same knife that was used to kill Sean Barber."

Calladine blinked. "They're different cases," he said. "I'm at a loss to understand that one." The inspector looked down at the body of the young woman. He'd only spoken to Frankie the previous day. Who had she upset so badly that she'd been murdered?

Natasha said, "There are marks around her throat, here." She pointed them out to Calladine. "They look to me like they were made by fingers pressing down hard."

Calladine pictured the scene. "There's a chase. Frankie can't get away. Her trainer slips off and she chucks it at her attacker. What then? He tries to strangle her?"

"CSI found some fibres on the barbed wire fence that runs around that rough ground," Natasha said. "Julian is testing them. He thinks they will match her top. If they do, the possibility is that she was held against the fence by the throat, and the knife thrust into her."

She wouldn't have stood a chance, thought Calladine. "She was all noise, this one. She couldn't put up much of a fight, there's nothing of her. I'll have a word with Julian before I leave."

"There's something else, Tom." Natasha looked at him, her expression hard. "She was pregnant. About ten weeks."

Calladine inhaled. Murder of an adult was bad enough, without killing the innocent and unborn too. "We could do with DNA. Finding out who fathered the child could be important."

"If he's on the database, no problem."

"How long had Frankie been dead before she was found?"

"No more than an hour."

"I've got a good reason to find her sister now. She needs to be told. Annie is the only close relative Frankie has."

Natasha nodded. "I'll write up the report and send it through before the end of the day."

Calladine left her to it and went to find Julian, who was in his lab. He looked up from his microscope and smiled as Calladine entered. Not like him at all.

"Check Frankie Halliwell's flat. Look for any sign of drugs. That seems to be the thread running through this investigation," Calladine said.

"There's a team on it now. Has Natasha told you about the fibres?"

"Yes, I've just seen her. But what I really need is a clue about who killed Frankie. I can't figure out why she had to die. She was on the periphery of this. It was Annie who was the main player."

Julian didn't answer. He seemed preoccupied. Then he said, "Are you okay, Tom, you know . . . with everything?"

Julian looked sheepish. The question was a reference to the baby, not the case.

Calladine smiled. "I'm fine with it, Julian. Zoe is a grown woman. I have no right to dictate what she does. Besides, a baby will be good for all of us."

"It'll be hard work." Julian turned back to his microscope. "But I'm sure we'll cope between us."

Calladine had a mental image of the baby being passed around like a parcel. They were all adults, but they all had demanding jobs. Initially Zoe would take maternity leave, but after that, well, who knew?

"Let me know what you find at Frankie's flat," said Calladine, returning to the matter at hand. "Also, get the techies to retrieve her phone data. I don't suppose you found any of her belongings at the crime scene?"

"No, we didn't. But I do have some other information for you." Julian reached over to a cabinet and took out a sheaf of papers. "Here's the report on Bill Geddes' clothes. No blood or anything else was found to suggest that Geddes killed Sean Barber. If he had stabbed the lad there would have been blood splatter, even if it was only tiny droplets. Also, we found traces of cocaine in his son Alex's flat. Most notably on the kitchen surfaces. If I had to hazard a guess, I'd say that's where they cut and packaged the stuff."

"Thanks, Julian. I'm pleased about Geddes. I interviewed him. He seemed like a decent man. Confused and grieving, but no killer."

Julian continued. "That laptop you gave the techies, the one belonging to Billy Alder. It was straightforward enough. The first email sent to Annie and the ransom demand sent to Alder were both sent from it. One of the technicians found them in the trash folder." Julian cleared his throat. "Not big on covering his tracks, was he? Conversely, Sean Barber's laptop has yielded nothing of interest."

Calladine headed back to his car. Frankie Halliwell and Sean Barber, what did they have in common? Nothing that he could see. It was a long shot, but he decided to have a word with Kat, see if Sean had ever spoken about Frankie.

"Tom!" A familiar voice called to him across the car park. "Nice bumping into you."

It was Doc Hoyle. "Hello! What are you doing here?" Calladine asked.

"Thought I'd have some lunch with Julian. He's in a better frame of mind these days. He's actually quite good company."

Calladine smiled. "Has he told you?"

"About the baby? Yes. I wasn't going to mention it because I wasn't sure if they'd told you yet. I said they should, and the sooner the better."

"It's a little strange — I'm still trying to get my head round it. I like Julian and all that, but from now on he'll be part of my family."

The doc laughed. "Families come in all shapes and sizes these days. Look at me and Margaret. We've been separated for years but never divorced. Technically, she's still my wife."

"But you still speak? You're civil to each other?"

"Of course. We even holidayed together last year. We had a great time. But she's best kept at arm's length."

The doc left Calladine in the car park, contemplating the thought of holidaying with Julian.

CHAPTER 24

Calladine gathered the team together in the incident room. "We've got two murders, linked we think by the fact that the killer used the same knife. But I'm at a loss to see what Sean Barber and Frankie Halliwell had in common. All we have is a nickname of the villain, 'Street,' but we've no idea who he is. None of the youngsters we've spoken to will tell us anything about him." Casting a wary eye towards the corridor to make sure Birch was nowhere in sight, he looked round the room. "Theories anyone?"

"Frankie and Sean could have upset the same dealer?" Alice postulated. "Drugs appear to be behind what's going on here."

"Not with the Alder case, it isn't," Calladine said. "And we don't have confirmation yet if Frankie was a user or not. Also, I've just been told by Dr Barrington that Frankie was pregnant. I'm hoping DNA on the foetus will give us the identity of the father."

"You don't think the father was Barber then?" Rocco asked.

"I've no idea. My instinct tells me no. But we need to know who Frankie's friends were, who she knocked around with."

"She was in love with Billy Alder, sir," Alice reminded him. "He led her on as a cover for his relationship with Annie. I'd say he was the prime suspect for father of the child."

Ruth inclined her head. "Could Billy have killed Sean and Frankie? Sean because of what he and the other kids were up to, and Frankie because she threatened his plans."

Alice nodded in agreement. "Frankie had texted Annie and threatened to tell Richard what was going on. Perhaps Billy silenced her?"

"It is possible that Billy had something to do with Frankie's murder, but he has no link to Sean that I'm aware of," Calladine told them. "How are we doing with finding out who 'Street' is?"

"No one will say a word," Rocco said. "Which is odd. Kids aren't usually so loyal."

Calladine thought for a moment. "Unless they are being threatened." There was a short pause while they mulled this over, then he caught Ruth's eye. "Or they don't know," he said, realising that she was thinking along the same lines as him.

"Dean Laycock is still in the cells," Ruth reminded him. "Let's find out if he's ever met 'Street' face to face."

"If he hasn't, then possibly none of them have. 'Street' could be anyone, not necessarily someone their own age."

Calladine got to his feet. "Ruth, you and Rocco speak to Laycock again. I'm going to have a word with Sean's mother, see if she can help with any of this."

* * *

Calladine decided to walk the short distance to Kat Barber's house. It was easier than struggling to find somewhere to park when he got there. She was still off work organising Sean's funeral, which was to be held at the end of the week.

"People have been very kind," she said. "The neighbours have organised a wake at the Wheatsheaf. One thing less to think about."

"Kat, do you know who Sean's friends were?"

She sighed heavily. "I know he was involved with those robbing little gits who were terrorising folk in their own homes. But to be honest, Sean was a bit of a loner. He knew the lads from his year in school, that's about it."

"Did he have a girlfriend?"

"God no! Who'd have him?" Calladine asked.

"Did he know Frankie Halliwell?"

"Alder's sister? I doubt it. Our Sean didn't mix with the likes of them."

"Frankie was Alder's wife's sister," he corrected her, "and she lived on the Hobfield. She didn't live in that big house. Frankie was simply a live-in guest from time to time."

"Well, my Sean didn't know her. She'd be older than him anyway."

"Are you sure?"

"Yes. He hadn't got round to girls yet, far too shy. Why are you so interested?"

"Because Frankie's been murdered. Stabbed, like Sean."

Kat looked shocked. "That's awful, but I can't help."

"Did Sean know Billy Alder?"

"No, I shouldn't think so. Billy isn't like his brother, he's more down to earth, but he wouldn't bother with the likes of our Sean."

Kat seemed very sure. However, she was still unaware that drugs had been found in Sean's bedroom. Perhaps that was the link. Perhaps Sean had been supplying both Billy and Frankie. "Did Sean seem okay in the days before he was killed? Did he say anything about what he was up to?"

"He told me nothing. I didn't even know he'd left the house that night he tried to rob you."

"Thanks, Kat. I'll keep you posted."

As he walked back to the station, Calladine rang Natasha at the Duggan for an update.

"Both Sean Barber and Frankie Halliwell were clean, Tom," she said. "No sign of drug taking."

Another dead end. But it begged the question, what was Sean doing with the drugs found in his bedroom — keeping them for someone?

* * *

Ruth sat down opposite Dean Laycock and his solicitor in the interview room. A uniformed officer positioned himself by the door.

"You okay, Dean?" Ruth tucked her injured right hand under the table. "Treating you well, are we?"

The lad replied with a grunt. "Wasting your time. I won't tell you owt."

Ruth gave him a smile. "Now, now, Dean, that's not very nice, is it? You don't know what we want yet."

"Piss off!"

Ruth ignored the remark. "This 'Street' you're all so fond of. Protect you in the same way, would he?" She asked. "You see, we're very close to nicking him and I bet when we do, we won't be able to shut him up. His lot are all the same. Look after number one and stuff the rest."

Laycock looked at her. She'd got his attention.

"Your little band has gone very quiet since the other night. Street won't like that. He'll blame you, Dean, for your stupid behaviour. You wouldn't want him on your back. Dangerous guy is Street."

"You've got him wrong. Street's alright."

"Was alright, you mean. He won't like the lull in trade. When did you last see him?"

"He texts me all the time."

"Are you saying he doesn't get his own hands dirty? That he doesn't join you all at your various venues? That's not fair. You and your mates are taking all the risks."

Dean gave a bored shrug. "Street said if we got into trouble with you lot, that he'd sort it."

Ruth glanced at James Delaney. Was the solicitor part of Street's 'sorting it'?

"When did you last see Street, Dean? It's a simple enough question."

Dean looked confused. "He texts. I've told you."

"What about face-to-face meetings?"

"No, not needed. Street reckons it's better we're not seen together."

"You've never actually set eyes on him, that's the truth of it, isn't it, Dean?"

"He got me 'im." Dean nodded at Delaney. "He's supposed to get me out."

"Not doing a very good job, is he?" Ruth said, ignoring the glare from the solicitor. "What d'you reckon Street is so afraid of? He won't show his face, so there must be something. Have you and your little gang discussed it?"

"He's alright, I've told you. Street won't let me down. He'll get me out. He knows people."

There was a determined look on Laycock's face. He was so sure, despite everything he had going against him.

"I'm afraid that's not how it works." Ruth gathered her paperwork together and stood up. "How often did Street contact you?"

"Every day at least."

"Busy little bunch, aren't you?" She smiled at Delaney. "Thank you, Dean. No doubt we'll talk again."

Back in the incident room Ruth briefed the team on what she'd learned. "I'll lay odds that none of that crew have ever actually seen this 'Street.' He could be anyone. I want Laycock's phone data. Street and he texted daily. That's something at least."

"Bet you won't find anything," Rocco told her. "This little gang are too well organised. They'll have burner phones. Laycock's probably got rid of his already."

"When we brought him in earlier today, he didn't have a phone on him." She looked at Rocco. "He was walking along the Hobfield Road. I reckon he saw the uniforms and ditched it. Get a search party out there and take a look."

CHAPTER 25

"I think Billy Alder found his cottage in mid-Wales," Alice announced. She'd had her head down for ages studying the newspapers they'd brought from Alf Alder's flat. "He's marked several adverts, but he's ringed one in particular and scribbled something beside it. I can't make out what, but it's for a property to let in an isolated spot by the Dovey estuary."

"Give the letting agents a ring," Calladine said. "See if they have names, and descriptions. We can't go chasing after them without solid information. If it checks out, we'll pay a visit."

Ruth looked up from her desk. "It's a long way to go, but given the seriousness of the case, we have no choice"

"Annie needs to be told about her sister. Given what's happened, she may be able to help. And we mustn't forget Billy. We have no idea where he was when Frankie was stabbed. He might still have been hanging around here. After the threats from Frankie, at the very least he's a person of interest."

Rocco burst into the incident room. "That villain's been released! I've just seen him leaving the building with his solicitor."

Ruth was furious. "Dean Laycock? How on earth does that happen? Who authorised this? I thought we were keeping him under wraps. He's been charged, hasn't he?"

Calladine had a pretty good idea what had happened. He went straight to Birch's office. "Laycock, why is he free? He tried to kill Ruth, he went for her with a knife. It was only down to her quick reaction that she's not lying in the morgue."

Birch frowned at the intrusion. "Don't be so melodramatic, Calladine," she scoffed. "I had no choice. I had to let him go."

"Has this come from Chesworth, ma'am?"

"Chief Superintendent Chesworth," she snapped back. "He's had a chat with the CPS and sees no reason to hold him."

Calladine could not believe what he was hearing. "That little bastard said Street would look out for him. He was confident that we wouldn't keep him for long."

"Rubbish! It's a technicality, that's all."

"What technicality? What's Chesworth's angle in this?"

"You're overreacting, Calladine. You forget, Isaac Chesworth is in charge now. He reads the reports and has the final say."

"We have a solid case, ma'am. Laycock attacked one of our officers. He should be punished."

"Who witnessed the attack?" she put to him. "The old man had left the house, he'd gone for Ruth's partner. So he's no use. None of Laycock's friends will testify. Ruth suffered a bang on the head. She was unconscious for some time. A good barrister would argue that her memory was faulty."

Calladine was aghast. "Is that Chesworth's argument?"

"Yes, and he makes a valid point. DCS Chesworth's orders were to let him go." She shrugged. "Get me more evidence and we'll try again."

Calladine had no idea what Birch or Chesworth were playing at, but there was little he could do for now. "We are looking for Annie Alder and Billy. We have a lead on where they might have gone."

Birch had her face buried in a pile of paperwork. At this news, her head shot up. "You're sure you've found them?"

"We're checking the detail."

"If it's them, don't say a word to anyone." She surprised him. "Not to their families or to anyone outside your team, understood?"

"Not even to Chesworth, ma'am?" he quipped sarcastically.

"No, particularly not to him."

* * *

Calladine returned to the incident room. The team were hard at it, going through each of the phone numbers in the papers Billy had made a mark against.

"Do you think Annie's friend, Joanne, will know anything?" Ruth asked him.

"It's worth a shot."

Alice was on the phone and gesturing for them to be quiet. "You're sure? And this was two days ago?"

"I think she's found them," Rocco whispered with a grin.

They team listened while Alice continued the conversation. Finally, she finished the call.

"A couple with a little girl took up the tenancy of a cottage on the Welsh coast a couple of days ago. The woman who checked them in gave her name as Wendy Jones — same as with the bank account. The descriptions match Annie and Billy, and the little girl's name is Sophie." Alice smiled.

Calladine was pleased. Alice had done well. "Send photos over to the local station and get them to check. Ask them not to scare them off. We don't want Annie and Billy doing another runner before we get there."

Ruth looked up. "Who's going?"

"Fancy a trip to Wales?"

"I've got a gammy hand."

130

"I'll drive. You can talk to Annie when we get there." He turned to the others. "Not a word about this outside this office." Heads nodded around the room.

"I'll go home in a bit and get ready," Ruth decided. "Do we have an actual address?"

Alice handed over a notepad.

"Ynyslas," Ruth nodded. "Lovely part of the world. That entire area is a nature reserve."

"You've been before, I take it?" said Calladine.

Ruth was a keen birdwatcher. "I went with the birding group, red kite spotting."

"We'll leave early and hope to get back the same day. But just in case, bring an overnight bag." He turned to Rocco. "Chase up forensics. We need to know who the father of Frankie's baby was."

"That's if he's known, guv. If not, what then?" Rocco asked.

"We'll deal with that as and when. Alice, find out what's happening locally regarding the kids. Monika at the care home will tell you if any more of her elderly folk are being terrorised. It's gone quiet on the vigilante front, too. Have a word with John Wells, and don't take any nonsense."

Calladine picked up the phone, despite Birch's instruction not to tell anyone, he wanted a word with Richard Alder. It was important that he didn't pay over the ransom money. "We may have found your wife and daughter. I'll be in touch within the next twenty-four hours to confirm. In the meantime, do not part with the money," he instructed.

"Given Annie has disappeared with my brother, I think you're right. She's let me down. She must feel pretty bad about our marriage to extort money out of me."

He was depressed, this had come as a huge shock. "Hold tight, we'll bring your child back," Calladine promised.

"Something's just come in, sir," Joyce called across the room. "Sean Barber's mobile phone, the one you found at his home. It's innocent enough. It more or less mirrors the data we have on the one lost at the scene. The numbers belong to friends and family."

"Check very carefully, Joyce. See if any of Sean's numbers match any in Laycock's data when it comes in."

"Yes, sir, the techies are still working on that," Joyce replied.

Rocco was on his mobile. "Uniforms have found the phone Dean Laycock discarded when he was brought in. Little sod threw it the other side of the hedge by the bus stop."

"Get it checked out. The data it holds might be useful."

"Like I said, guv, these phones are cheap with prepaid sims fitted. The gang use them for a few days and then they're discarded."

"Clever little buggers, aren't they?"

Rocco shrugged. "It's big business, drug dealing. Whoever is at the top of this dung heap can afford it."

CHAPTER 26

Kat Barber had made a real effort. She was wearing makeup and had had her hair done. The effect was pleasing on the eye, but made Calladine nervous. What was the woman after? If it was anything other than neighbourly friendship, she was out of luck. He wasn't ready to embark on a new relationship yet. He'd just split up with one women, after all.

"The funeral's Friday," she said. "Will you come?"

Calladine nodded and got a smile in response. "We're still looking for Sean's killer," he said. "We have a strong lead and we're waiting for forensics to give us a name."

"I've been thinking about what you said. Particularly the way Sean was these last few weeks."

"What d'you mean, Kat?"

"He wasn't himself. He went around with the same lads, occasionally went to work, but there was something up." She went to the sideboard. "I found this in his denim jacket." She handed Calladine a small notebook. "I think someone was leaning on him, making him do stuff. I'm aware he was no angel, but just lately he went from bad to worse. He was moody, out all hours too."

Calladine was curious. Where had the book come from. "I thought we searched Sean's room?"

"His jacket was in the wash basket. No one asked about it and I forgot."

Calladine flipped through the book. It was full of names and addresses, all of them from around the Greater Manchester area. He recognised Mr Hopkins, Ruth's neighbour. And then he spotted his own name and address. Suddenly he realised what the book was about. This was Sean clocking likely candidates for the cuckooing scam. Did the wide area covered by the book mean that this was much bigger than they'd realised? Map these addresses on a chart and they'd fan out from Leesdon like a spider's web across Leesworth, and beyond. On the back inside cover was a mobile phone number. Next to it was one word — 'Street.' His stomach did a somersault. This could be the break they needed.

"How did Sean get about?" he asked Kat.

"He had a car."

Calladine hadn't even known that Sean could drive. "How did he afford that?"

Kat sighed and shook her head. "I don't know, and I didn't ask. Things were always better that way with Sean. But it was no cheap job. It's the black Audi lying burnt out on the Hobfield car park."

"How did that happen?"

"I've no idea. He got a call, went storming off one night and when he came home, he said someone had trashed his car."

"Did he report it?"

She looked scornful. "Who'd be interested? Your lot have taken no notice. It's standing there, a burnt-out hulk, and not one of you lot has questioned it."

"How often did he use it?"

"Often enough, went all over. Those pals of his used him as a taxi driver most of the time."

Calladine would get forensics to take a look. He held up the notebook. "I'm sorry, Kat, this is important. I'm going to have to return to the station. There's information in here my team should know about. Someone will come and take the car away. It'll have to be examined."

"Do I keep the food hot?"

"Look, I could be some time, and I'm away for a couple of days from tomorrow."

"Okay, I get it. You don't have to say anymore."

Kat Barber looked disappointed. Calladine didn't want to upset the woman, but he didn't want her getting the wrong idea either. Time to put her straight. "I'm investigating the murder of your son, Kat. Our relationship has to be a professional one. Anything else and I risk my job."

* * *

It was gone eight at night and the team had gone home. Alone in the incident room, Calladine sat at his desk and went through Sean's notebook one page at a time.

Apart from his own, there were six other names and addresses he recognised. Those from the different areas would have to be checked out. He'd get uniform on the job. A visit to each address, have a word with the residents and ensure they were okay and knew the score. The phone number for 'Street' was another matter. He rang the technicians at the Duggan.

"I have a mobile number I want tracing," he began. "It's a long shot. No doubt it'll turn out to be a pay-as-you-go and the owner can't be found, but I'd like you to try."

Calladine read out the number. After a moment the technician told him that the phone was turned off. "We'll monitor it closely," he promised.

"The individual it belongs to is involved in a murder enquiry. When it is turned on, let me know at once. You've looked at data on another suspect's phone, Sean Barber. Does that number appear on the list?"

There was a short silence while the technician checked. "We've just compiled the list, sir, and yes, it does. Both

Laycock and Barber phoned the number. Laycock once and Barber three times."

That must have been when they didn't have use of a disposable. Calladine made another call, this time to Julian. Despite the hour, he too was still working.

"I should have the DNA results from Frankie Halliwell soon," Julian said.

"Me and Ruth are taking a trip to Wales tomorrow, but ring me when they're in. Sean Barber had a car," Calladine continued. "It was set alight a while ago and is currently parked in the Hobfield car park. It's an Audi. Get it examined. I want to know if there is any trace of drugs."

"Will do. Why Wales?"

Calladine trusted Julian, if he told him to keep this quiet, he would. "We believe that's where Annie Alder is. Now that her sister's dead, I could do with a word with her, but not a word to anyone. This is very much under the radar. If it gets out, she may be in danger."

Once he'd finished speaking to Julian, Calladine left a note for Rocco telling him about the notebook and Sean's car. He instructed the DC to contact their colleagues in the other areas listed in the notebook and give them the heads-up. The only problem now was what to tell Birch. Nothing, he decided. Her reticence to go after Street meant she couldn't be trusted.

CHAPTER 27

Day 6

Calladine and Ruth were on the road by seven a.m. Calladine had no choice but to drive as Ruth's hand was still heavily bandaged.

"What d'you reckon Birch is up to?" she asked. "Why on earth would she tell you to lay off Street?"

"She has no choice. She's under orders from Chesworth," Calladine replied.

"So what's going on?"

"I've no idea. I can see no reason why Chesworth would do this."

"Don't give me that. You've prattled on for the last twenty miles about it. You must have a theory."

Calladine stared out of the windscreen, concentrating on the road. "Honestly, I'm clueless on this one. Every time I mention the name 'Street' she tells me to leave it."

"What's Chesworth up to? He has no idea what goes on in Leesworth at ground level."

"Birch says he's reading the statements and reports as they come in. Why he's so interested is a mystery. Oldston has far more on its hands currently. It is possible that Street is an informant, but he'd have to be a pretty important one to merit the protection he's getting."

"There could be another reason," Ruth said. "What if Chesworth is being paid to 'make things go away'?"

"Surely we've not got another one! Ford was a serial killer and now you're suggesting that Chesworth is on the take. We don't have much luck, do we!"

"But you can't be sure, can you? None of us have actually worked with him."

"No one's said anything."

"I've heard something," Ruth admitted. "I didn't tell you because it sounded a bit far-fetched to me."

Calladine glanced across at her. "Come on then, out with it."

"Rumour has it that one of the senior officers in the Greater Manchester area is on the payroll of some big villain. Whoever this is has only recently started protecting this individual. And where does Chesworth come from, the Central Manchester force."

"In what way protecting?"

"You know the sort of stuff, losing paperwork, pointing the finger elsewhere. Ensuring lowly inspectors don't cock it up."

"And you think this senior officer is Chesworth? Hardly likely. Surely he would be under suspicion by now."

"This is recent, Tom, and you don't know that he isn't," Ruth pointed out. "Birch might not even know."

Calladine wasn't convinced. He might not know the man, but he knew Chesworth had been around for years, climbed through the ranks. "He's been a superintendent for a good while. He doesn't earn peanuts. What makes you think it's Chesworth, anyway?"

"I don't. I'm simply putting together what you've said with the stuff I've heard. And don't ask who the villain is either, 'cos I've no idea. But it could be why he doesn't want this 'Street' upsetting."

"Street isn't the big villain. We'd have heard the name before. Whoever he is, Street is new."

"Or perhaps an established villain with a new persona for this particular job."

Ruth had a point. "Why would he need a new persona?"

"Think about it, Tom. He's dealing with the younger end. 'Street' is the sort of name they'd remember, think was cool."

Calladine nodded. She was onto something. None of the kids had actually met this 'Street.' He was a name that appeared on their phones and gave out the orders. He could be anybody.

"Are we nearly there yet? I'm getting cramp in my backside," Calladine moaned.

"You're like a kid, you are. Satnav says about ten miles until we reach Aberystwyth."

"Then what?"

"Along the coast to Borth, and then it's only a short hop to Ynyslas. There aren't many dwellings there, so the cottage should be easy to find."

Calladine's mobile rang. "Can you get that?" he asked Ruth.

She picked up the phone. "Hi, Julian, it's Ruth. Tom's driving, so I'll put you on speakerphone."

The forensic scientist's voice filled the car. "We've gone over Sean Barber's Audi. Someone has had a go at setting it alight, but they didn't do a thorough job. We found no trace of drugs. However, we did find something — a knife taped underneath the driver's seat. It was placed there after the car was burnt. It was wrapped in a plastic bag and the blade is still intact."

The news surprised Calladine. He didn't have Sean down as the type to use a knife. "Fingerprints?"

"We're working on that. It's got a long narrow blade. Someone's had a go at cleaning it but we'll test it against Sean and Frankie's blood. It could be the murder weapon. Also, the car isn't registered in Sean Barber's name. I presume the plates are false. We will look at the VIN number and see what we get."

"Thanks, Julian, interesting information. I'll have a word with his mother about the car when we get back. See what she knows."

* * *

The Welsh countryside was impressive. Green rolling hills that swept down to the wide estuary below. The sands around Borth were golden and flat. The weather was fine, with only a light breeze blowing across the low dunes.

"You can see right across the estuary," Ruth said, binoculars in hand. "Over there, at the point where the River Dovey runs down from the hillside is Dovey Junction railway station. Way back in Victorian times an entrepreneur tried to bridge this estuary and failed, so they had to go all the way round." She looked up. Calladine's eyes had glazed over. "It's a fascinating story!" She punched him playfully. "It brought industry and the railway to this part of the country. If you ever get the chance, take a ride along the Cambrian coast from Dovey Junction to Pwllheli. The views are beautiful."

He rolled his eyes. "You've been here before, you said?"

"Yes birding. We stayed in a little hotel in Borth. I've walked all over these sands."

"Do you know this address?" He handed her Alice's notepad.

"Brickyard Cottages?" She looked around at the expanse of sand and estuary. "All that industry I talked about meant Borth grew — it needed a railway station for starters. That required builders and they need bricks." She pointed. "See that white farmhouse over there?" Calladine followed the direction of her finger and nodded. "That was once the old brickyard. There is a row of cottages at the back. I'm guessing it's them."

"What's the farm called now?"

"Dovey Farm."

"It was the owner of that farm who let the cottage to Annie and Billy."

Ruth put her binoculars back in her bag. "There's just one problem. How do we get over there without them spotting us?"

* * *

Calladine and Ruth decided to chance being seen. They pulled into the farm car park. A middle-aged woman was returning from walking a couple of dogs. She called to them in Welsh.

"*Bore da, I helpu chi?*"

"That means, good morning, can I help you," Ruth translated for Calladine's benefit.

"Do you speak English?" Calladine asked, showing the woman his warrant card.

"Yes, of course. I'm Delyth Hughes. I own this farm and the land around here."

"We need to find the couple who recently rented a cottage from you. You spoke to one of my colleagues yesterday."

"The Jones family? Yes, I know them. They took on number five, the cottage on the end of the row there."

"Are they in?" Ruth asked.

"I've just walked past and the car is still there. I'd say you're in luck." Delyth left them to it.

"We'll walk round," Calladine told Ruth. "If we approach from the back, then hopefully they won't see us."

"They're hardly going to do a runner."

"We don't know that Billy isn't the killer," Calladine reminded her. "Until we know different, we go carefully."

CHAPTER 28

As the two detectives approached the rear of the cottage, they could see little Sophie Alder playing on the lawn outside.

"Despite all our theories, seeing her safe and well is a huge relief," Ruth said.

"Led us a merry dance though, didn't they, Annie and Billy?"

The pair accessed the garden by a small gate in the fence. Ruth waved at the child and gave her a big grin. Sophie went running inside, no doubt to find her mother.

"What d'you want?" A male voice boomed from behind them. It was Billy Alder. He was carrying an axe. "I'm chopping wood for the stove," he explained, throwing it to the ground.

"We need a word with you and Annie. Is she here?" Calladine asked.

Billy didn't look happy but nonetheless he led the way inside. The place was sparsely furnished, nothing like the luxury Annie Alder was used to.

She was in the kitchen, clutching Sophie. She went paled when she saw the two detectives.

"We've done nothing wrong," she said at once. "I had to do it this way or Rick would have killed us both." She put

Sophie down and instructed the child to go and play in her bedroom. "You have no idea what he's capable of. Richard is nothing like people think, and now that he's got Pennington at his side, he's even worse."

"Tell us, Annie. Tell us the truth about your husband," Calladine pressed her. "If we are to help you, we need the full picture."

"There's a lot I could say, but it boils down to one fact. Rick is a dangerous man, and Pennington is every bit as bad as he is."

"If you want us to help you, we need more than that. We need details. What do you mean by dangerous? What has he done to make you believe this?"

"I can't tell you," she said. "We're safe here, but if Rick finds out that I've spoken to you, he'll find us." She dipped her head. "He'll come after us and it won't be pretty."

"You have to trust us," Ruth said. "We won't tell anyone where you are."

"You won't have to. You write reports, your senior officers know what you're up to, where you've been." She gave a hollow laugh. "I don't trust anyone. Particularly not the police."

Calladine thought that was an odd thing to say.

"We can protect you all. Find you a safe house. Help us and no one will find you, we promise," said Ruth.

"This was a safe house, until you found us. I can't take any more risks. Not while Rick is glued to Pennington."

"You think Pennington is dangerous too?"

"Let's just say that since they've been together, Rick has changed, and not for the better."

"Has he known Pennington for long?" Calladine asked.

"A year, no more. I've no idea where or how they met. I have asked Rick, but he won't tell me. He's closer to him than to his own brother." She glanced at Billy, who remained silent.

Ruth moved closer. "Something has happened, Annie," she said gently. "It's Frankie, and I'm afraid it's not good news."

"Had an accident, has she? The way she drives that car of hers it wouldn't surprise me."

There was no other way but straight out with it. "No. I'm afraid Frankie has been killed. Murdered. That's why we're here. We're trying to find the person responsible."

Annie froze, then her face crumpled as she burst into tears. "Why would anyone hurt Frankie?" she sobbed. "I don't understand. She's my sister. I need her."

"I'm so sorry, Annie. We are investigating and we will find her killer soon."

Annie glowered at Ruth. "You say that, but here you are chasing after us, not back at home chasing her killer."

"We had to come. We needed to tell you what happened."

Annie nodded in resignation. "Yes. Of course. Sorry."

"Did you know Frankie was pregnant?"

Annie's eyes widened at this news. "There hasn't been a man in her life for a while."

"Well, there was someone. She was about ten weeks, does that help?"

"How did she die?" Annie asked, ignoring the previous question.

"She was stabbed."

There was an uncomfortable silence as Annie sobbed.

"When did you get here, Billy?" Calladine asked, turning to the man.

Billy scowled. "I didn't kill her, if that's what you're getting at."

"Surely you can't suspect Billy! He wouldn't harm anyone!" Annie shouted. "And certainly not my sister." She thought for a moment. "Have you asked Rick? He never did like Frankie. She got on his nerves. She went on and on at him about what he did to me . . ." She looked at them both. "When Rick loses it, he's a wild man. Nothing would surprise me."

"Has he ever hurt you, Annie?" Ruth asked. She was thinking about the bruise on her cheek.

Annie's hand went to her cheek, as if reading Ruth's thoughts. "Yes. He's had a short fuse lately. Frankie always took my side and Rick didn't like that."

"Proof of when you got here would clear this up," Calladine told them. "You see, we know that Frankie sent you a text threatening to tell Richard what your plans were. You've just told us you didn't want him on your tails while you were making your escape." He paused. "As it stands, you have a motive for wanting Frankie dead. Keeping your whereabouts a secret, for example."

There was doubt on Annie's face. "Frankie said a lot of things. She gets drunk, flies off the handle. But she didn't mean any of what she texted. She knew the score with Rick. She knew I had to leave."

"Couldn't you have simply asked him for a divorce?" Ruth asked.

"I did. I pleaded with him, but he refused. And he promised I wouldn't get a penny or access to Sophie if I walked out. That just isn't fair! I worked damn hard helping him to get that business up and running. I wanted that money because I'd earned it." Annie sighed. "Billy came away with Sophie and me two days ago. He didn't harm Frankie. Neither of us could do that."

Billy spoke. "Here, take these and do all the checking you want." He handed Calladine a couple of petrol receipts. They were dated and timed the day before Frankie's murder.

"Most garages have CCTV, so it shouldn't be hard to check. Plus, Mrs Hughes will confirm what I say."

Calladine turned to Annie. "Apart from your husband, who would want to harm your sister?"

He saw Annie and Billy exchange a look. From the expression on Annie's face, it was obvious that she knew a lot more than she was saying.

"Tell us what you know, Annie," Calladine pushed. "Frankie isn't the only person this man has killed. We have to stop him before he strikes again. All we need is a name."

"I can't," she sobbed. "You won't get him, anyway. He's untouchable."

"Tell us, Annie," Ruth urged her. "Who do you think killed Frankie? She was your sister, you owe it to her to tell us."

"I can't. He'll kill us."

"Who will? Richard?"

Annie stood up and turned her back on them. "Please go. I daren't say anymore."

"What makes you say he's untouchable?" Calladine persisted.

"Because he's got people to watch his back."

"What d'you mean, Annie? Are you talking about Pennington?"

"I can't help you. Please go. Please leave us alone."

"That's not good enough," Calladine said firmly. "If you suspect someone then you have to speak out. Refuse and I'll arrest you here and now for obstruction."

Annie Alder turned to face him with cold eyes. "My husband and Pennington. That's who killed Frankie. They have secrets, the way they make money for starters. Frankie saw through them and Rick couldn't stand her. She was always making trouble for him."

"Do you have proof?" Ruth asked.

Annie shook her head. "No. And I'm not saying anything else. I've said too much as it is."

"You will have to make the funeral arrangements for Frankie, so you risk Richard finding you anyway," Ruth said. "We can help, but you have to help us in return."

"I'll get Joanne to make the arrangements for me. I'm not saying anything else. It's too dangerous, and I've got Sophie to think of."

There was nothing they could do. Annie had a fixed expression on her face and it was clear they would get no more information out of her. It was frustrating. Calladine wanted to know why she thought her husband was a murderer. They had no proof or any reason to believe that.

He decided to leave it for now, but they'd have another go tomorrow before they left.

"Okay, Annie," he said calmly. "But you will speak to us. Your safety depends on it."

* * *

"Where're we staying, then?" Calladine asked Ruth once they were back in the car. They had decided to stay over and try again with Annie the following day.

"There's the hotel in Borth I told you about. Great breakfast, lovely views, and a well-stocked bar."

"Sounds the business. D'you think they'll have rooms?"

"I know the owner, Bethan Thomas. The birding group have stayed there in the past. You drive us back to Borth and on the way I'll give her a ring."

The hotel was everything Ruth had promised. Old and quaint, but very comfortable.

"Knew it would be fine," Ruth said as they checked in. She nudged Calladine and pointed at the range of whiskeys behind the bar. "We've had many a good night in here."

He was impressed. "I need to make a few calls. I'll meet you back down here for dinner."

One of the calls was to Rocco. Calladine wanted to make sure he had the information he'd requested on Sean Barber's car. "Julian made the initial enquires but I want you to dig a bit deeper. Where did Sean get that car from? There was a knife strapped under the driver's seat. Sean may or may not have known it was there. If he did, he could have had it with him when he was stabbed, and the killer then put it there."

"We'll get on it, guv. We've also had the forensics back on Frankie's murder. They've found a match on the database for the foetal DNA."

"Do you have a name?" Calladine asked.

"Conrad Stokes."

It was something of an anti-climax. He'd half expected it to be Billy Alder. The name Stokes meant nothing to Calladine.

"There's more, guv. Forensics proved that the killer stabbed both Frankie and Sean Barber. They found faint traces of Sean's blood in Frankie's wound. It must have been close to the hilt of the blade. But tests on the blade are ongoing, as you know. With luck it'll prove to be the murder weapon in both cases."

"Good, just as we thought. Just wish we knew who Stokes was, then we might make headway."

"Already on it," Rocco said. "Stokes is on the system. He's some big-time Glaswegian villain. Used to be responsible for most of the organised crime up there, particularly drug dealing. The Scottish police were very helpful, they sent a profile and a photo. I've emailed them to you. It'll make interesting bedtime reading. The photo was taken a decade or so ago. According to the Glaswegian force, Stokes has been out of circulation for a while."

But Calladine couldn't wait. He took the laptop from his bag and fired it up. "Have you seen much of Birch today?" he asked the DC.

"No, guv. In fact, I don't think she was here. Thorpe's being a pain. Doesn't want to leave the office if it can be avoided."

The hotel had Wi-Fi and Calladine accessed the email from Rocco. Seconds later an image of Stokes filled the screen. "I don't know him. Mind you that's some beard he's got, and his hair's quite long. Wonder what he looks like spruced up? Drugs you said? He could be behind the current drug problem we have. In fact, he could be our 'Street.' You'll have seen Sean's notebook — the problem is bigger than we thought and that takes some organising. Stokes is an old hand according to the profile."

"Do you think he killed Frankie and Sean Barber, guv?"

"He has to be our number one suspect. What with the drug link, and the fact that he's the father of Frankie's child, so he knew her."

"What next?" Rocco asked.

"I want another crack at Annie and Billy. Annie is holding back on us. But at least we can put Billy on the back burner for now."

"You think she's scared of her husband? Not the Richard Alder we know though, is he?"

"She hasn't spoken of anyone else," Calladine said. "Any further information turns up, let me know at once."

Calladine ended the call. If Stokes was their man then the two murders may have nothing to do with Richard Alder or Giles Pennington, despite what Annie thought.

* * *

The dinner Bethan Thomas provided was every bit as good as Ruth had promised. Comfortably full, the pair retired to the bar.

"I've not been to this part of the world before," said Calladine. "It's quite a find, particularly if you fancy a bit of peace and quiet."

Ruth smiled. "Not when the birding group's here it isn't. And not just us — word gets out about a sighting and the twitchers travel from miles away."

"Bethan does well out of you lot then."

Ruth changed the subject. "The team got anything yet?"

"The father of Frankie's baby is a man called Conrad Stokes, from Glasgow. He needs finding and bringing in."

Ruth nodded. "Do you think this Stokes could be 'Street'?"

"I was thinking that too. But all we know for sure is that he's a drug dealer."

"Talking about babies," Ruth said. "How's Zoe doing?"

Calladine took a swig of his whiskey before replying. "She's fine. You know, looking forward to the big event."

He coughed and looked away. Discussing Zoe, in view of what he knew about Julian, could become a problem. Ruth was bound to notice the difference in the man and wonder what the reason behind it was. Calladine could do without the speculation.

"I know something," he admitted. "A secret for the time being, but it won't stay that way for long."

"About the baby?" Ruth was intrigued. "Go on, you can't leave it like that. What secret?"

"It's about the baby's father."

Calladine saw Ruth's face light up. "You know who he is, don't you?"

He nodded. "You will never guess, not in a million years."

"If Zoe knows him then you probably do too." She thought for a moment. "I'm too tired to work it out. Come on Calladine, spill."

He saw no reason to hold back. "Julian."

Ruth stared at him in amazement. "Our Julian? You're right, I would never have guessed. How did that happen?"

"All organised by the IVF clinic, apparently. You were right, they just took their own donor along."

"I bet Julian loved that!"

Calladine shook his head. "You know what this means? Julian is forever stapled to me and my family. I'm not sure how I feel about that." He looked at Ruth. "There's Amy to consider, too. She's coming for a visit and she'll want to be involved with the baby."

Ruth gave him a broad smile. "You're worrying for no reason. You like Amy. The pair of you get along just fine. Julian's a good bloke and once he gets the hang of things, I'm sure he'll make a super dad. I take it he wants to be hands-on?

"Very much so, according to Zoe."

"It's Jo I feel for. Think about it. Zoe is carrying the child, Julian is its dad. She's bound to feel a little left out. Biologically, the infant has nothing to do with her."

"Zoe and Jo have a strong relationship, they'll cope. They'll have to."

"Can I have a word?" A gruff male voice interrupted.

It was Billy Alder. His sudden appearance at the bar surprised both detectives. "Sit down," Calladine offered. "Want a drink?"

Alder refused both. "I want you to leave Annie alone. She can't take any more. Annie isn't a strong woman. After life with my brother, she's a nervous wreck."

"I'd like nothing more than to do just that," Calladine assured him. "But I think Annie is holding back. She didn't tell us the truth about Sophie. She had us running around looking for a missing child, remember?"

"She's explained that. It was the only way we could escape from Rick. He'd never have let her have Sophie"

"Do you know a man called Conrad Stokes?" Calladine wanted to see his reaction.

Billy took a step back. He looked from Calladine to Ruth in turn, as if trying to weigh up what they knew. "No. Why, should I?"

"I've no idea, but his name has come up. Do you think Annie might know him?"

"No!"

He answered too fast for Calladine's liking. "I find that odd, Billy. You see, Frankie knew him. The sisters will have spoken, shared confidences."

"You know nothing," Billy said. "Frankie was good at keeping secrets. From now on, stay away from us, or you'll regret it."

CHAPTER 29

Day 7

"Have they got anything?" Alice asked after Rocco put the phone down. He'd been talking to Calladine about yesterday's events.

Rocco shook his head. "It's more of a 'to do' list. Do we know who Frankie's friends were?"

"Yes, but she didn't hang out with them much. They're mostly people she knew at school or college," Alice said.

"Boyfriends?"

"The only one we know about is Billy Alder, and that was all one-sided."

"So how did she know Conrad Stokes? Their paths must have crossed at some point."

"Perhaps on a night out?" Alice suggested.

"So where is he now? Where does he live, work? Someone must know this man. Tracking back through Frankie's movements might help. We need to know where Frankie went and who she was with during the last couple of months. Others might know about this Stokes." He waved Sean Barber's notebook at her. "The answer might be in here. Trouble is, there are just so many names and addresses."

"They're the potential victims of the cuckooing scam," Alice reminded him. "Not those involved. If Stokes is 'Street,' then he's behind that scam too. Perhaps Frankie found out."

"DC Rockliffe." It was a uniformed PC from downstairs. "We've got a situation. Bill Geddes is downstairs asking for DI Calladine. He's got a young lad with him and won't let him go."

"What d'you mean?"

"Geddes has him by the scruff of his neck and is refusing to release him. I thought it best to come and get one of you lot."

Rocco was intrigued. He followed the PC down to reception and found a right ruck going on. A young lad was kicking and shouting, but Geddes would not release him.

"Here, he's all yours." Geddes hurled the lad at Rocco, sending him slipping across the tiled floor on his backside. "Little runt was setting up a bloody drug den in a mate's house, just like they did with my Alex."

Geddes chucked a sports bag at Rocco. "Full of white powder. Cocaine, I reckon."

Rocco took a quick look inside the bag. Geddes was right. "Is this a vigilante thing?"

"No, it's a looking out for your neighbour thing. Pity no one did the same for my son." Geddes dusted himself down and turned for the door. "Found him on Clough Road," he said on his way out.

Rocco looked at the lad. He didn't recognise him. "Name?"

"Get lost!"

"Lock him up. Better put this somewhere safe, too." He handed the bag over to the uniform.

Rocco went back upstairs. "We've got a fortune in cocaine stashed downstairs. God knows where the kids are getting it from."

Alice looked up from her computer. "They're shifting it, too. Alex Geddes, Rowena Hargreaves, and the old chap who lives up near Ruth. Goodness knows how many more. That's a lot of gear. It's getting into the area somehow."

"According to the boss, this Stokes is a well-known dealer from Glasgow. It's too much of a coincidence that we've got this drug problem and he's in the area. We need to find him."

Alice frowned. "The only thing we've got is that profile the Glasgow police sent us."

"We know he was hanging out around the Hobfield. That's where he killed Frankie."

"Who's the kid Geddes brought in?" Alice asked.

"Wouldn't give his name."

"Want to have a go at him?"

"I'll ring Calladine first."

* * *

"We've another one in custody, guv," Rocco said. "This time we've got the drugs too, all thanks to Bill Geddes."

Calladine shook his head. Even after the killings and the police involvement, it hadn't stopped. "They're a brazen lot," he said. Someone was making them believe they're untouchable.

Calladine frowned. Were they being protected by a high-ranking police officer? It was not a comforting thought.

"We'll have another word with Annie and then hit the road," he told Rocco. "We need to get back to Leesdon."

Ruth and Calladine drove the short distance back to the cottages in Ynyslas. Annie and Billy's place was locked up tight, doors shut and curtains drawn. "I hope they've not done another runner," Calladine groaned. "What is it they're so scared of?"

"Richard Alder's revenge," Ruth replied.

"So take him through the courts, get an injunction, accept our protection. She's his wife, she's entitled to something out of their marriage. She has options, she doesn't have to run."

Delyth Hughes walked across the yard to meet them. "They've gone. Thanks for that." She was cross. "Seems you scared them off. Shame, they were a nice family."

"Do you know where they went?" asked Calladine.

"No. I asked, in case any mail comes for them, but they refused to say."

Ruth sighed. "So much for that. Bit of a wasted journey."

"Do you mind if we take a look around the cottage?"

"Help yourself." Delyth handed them the key.

"She blames us," Ruth whispered as Delyth left. "Apart from holiday lets, I bet this is a difficult place to get tenants for."

"We can't worry about that, we've got a job to do."

The pair went inside. It looked very much as Annie and Billy must have found it, little in the way of furniture but clean and tidy.

"Take a look upstairs," Calladine told Ruth. He wandered around, opening drawers and cupboards. There was nothing to suggest where they'd gone.

"They must have had phones," Calladine said to Ruth when she came back. "Annie said Joanne would help sort out Frankie's funeral. If Annie makes contact, we might catch up with her again. We'll get her mobile data once we're back."

"Good idea," said Ruth. "But I don't think Annie will miss Frankie's funeral, Tom. They were sisters. She'll make the effort, danger or not."

Calladine continued his search in the kitchen. The cupboards and drawers were empty. He put on a pair of latex gloves and tentatively lifted the lid on the rubbish bin. There wasn't much, an old newspaper and some empty bottles. Then he spotted it. Lying at the bottom was a sheet of paper. Calladine lifted it out. It was a registration document for a car, a black Audi. The name of the registered keeper was Giles Pennington.

CHAPTER 30

Rocco and Alice sat in the interview room opposite the young lad who'd been brought in by Bill Geddes. With him was the solicitor, James Delaney. A uniformed PC stood in the corner.

"This is costing someone a fortune," Rocco quipped as they readied themselves. "Twice in one week. Business is good."

Delaney didn't reply.

"Your name?" Rocco asked the lad.

The boy nudged Delaney, who nodded in response.

"Andrew Harvey," came the sullen reply.

"How old are you, Andrew?" Alice asked with a smile.

"What's it to you?"

"We need to determine if we should get your parents down here," she explained.

"I'm nineteen, and they're not interested."

"Are you sure? I could ring your mum, ask her to come in."

"Do one, copper!"

Rocco had written the lad's name on a pad and handed it to the PC. "See what's known."

"Are you sure you don't want your mum here, Andrew? It might help to know that she's waiting for you."

The lad scowled. "She threw me out. Believe me, she's not interested."

"Where did you get the sports bag from, Andrew?" Rocco asked. He wanted to get on with this. Whether the lad had a parent here or not didn't interest him.

"It weren't mine. It were a set-up. That bloke shoved it in my arms and dragged me in here."

"Is that a fact? The gentleman who brought you in told us he picked you up on Clough Road. We can easily check both your stories. There's plenty of CCTV cameras around there."

The lad's eyes narrowed. "You ain't pinning this on me."

"Who should we pin it on then, Andrew?" Rocco asked. "Your friend Street, maybe?"

The lad swore under his breath. "Don't know him. And that stuff weren't mine."

"What stuff? Do you know what was in the bag?"

"Bloke that brought me in said it were cocaine." He shrugged. "I thought it was my mate's sports gear."

"You knew very well what that bag contained," Rocco said sharply. "What mate?"

The lad smirked. "Forget his name."

"Would you like to tell us about your little gang?" Alice asked. "It doesn't seem fair that you should take the rap all on your own."

"I'm no grass."

"No, but you want to save your own skin, I'll bet. You see, Andrew, if we don't get any more names, you'll be charged and take the blame for the lot. It's in your interest to talk to us. Stay silent, and it won't help your case. You'll go down for a very long time."

Andrew leaned back in his chair. "That won't happen. I'll be out later today, you'll see."

Rocco stared at the lad. He was worryingly confident about that, he even had a smirk on his face. After what had happened with Laycock, Rocco was concerned. "What makes you think that?"

The lad shrugged. "Know folk, don't we."

"What folk, Andrew? Tell me about them."

The lad turned to Delaney. "I've got a headache. The bloke who dragged me in here knocked me about."

"My client would like a drink and time to recover," Delaney announced. "He can't think straight after suffering at that man's hands."

"Okay. Take him back to the cells and get him something to eat and drink," Rocco told the PC.

When they were alone, Rocco slammed the file onto the desk. He hadn't shown it during the interview, but he was seething. "They're playing us, Alice! He'll walk just like Dean Laycock, and there isn't a damn thing we can do about it."

* * *

Ruth and Calladine drove in silence for several miles. Calladine was trying to work out what the registration document meant. Billy Alder had obviously left it for them — but why? The only reason Calladine could think of was to point the finger.

Ruth broke the silence. "Giles Pennington? Why him? Apart from being Richard Alder's new best chum, he's an unknown."

"But is he? Did we ever get the background on him? Where is he living, for instance?"

"I don't know. I'll need to speak to Alice."

"Ring Rocco. Give him the VIN number off that document and get him to check the burnt-out car. Ask him to chase up Pennington's background while you're at it."

"If we are to believe everything Annie and Billy told us about Richard, perhaps Pennington is involved somehow."

"I think he might be involved with the drug dealing. Hence Sean having his car."

"Sean could have stolen it," Ruth pointed out. "And what about the knife? Did that belong to Sean or Pennington?"

"According to his mother, Sean went everywhere in that car. He wasn't afraid to be seen in it, so I don't think he stole it. If Sean was stabbed with that knife and it was his, how did it end up taped to the underside of the driver's seat after it was burnt? Too many puzzles, Ruth. I need to think."

Calladine pulled into a lay-by. "You ring Rocco, I'll have a word with Kat."

Calladine got out of the car to make the call. Kat picked up at once. "Quick question," he began. "That car of Sean's, where did he get it?"

"He came home with it one night. Said he'd been given it for work."

"The building job?"

"No, it was before that, when he was doing a stint up at the biscuit factory."

Calladine had no idea Sean had worked there, but what Kat had told him made sense. "Did he know Richard Alder or any of his colleagues?"

"Our Sean? I doubt it. He didn't stay up there long enough to get to know anyone."

"And the car? No one came looking?"

"No, he parked it across the road and drove it most days. He can't have nicked it, if that's what you think. The police would have stopped him."

She was right. "Thanks, Kat. Speak soon."

That was all very well, but surely the car should have gone back to Alder's factory when the job came to an end.

"Rocco isn't happy," said Ruth, joining him. "The lad Geddes brought in with the drugs thinks he'll be released too. He's not taking any of it seriously. What's going on, Tom? These kids think they're above the law. We bring them in, they laugh it off and within a couple of hours — they walk."

Calladine wanted answers. "I'm going to speak to Birch." He took out his phone again and rang the DCI's direct number. "Ma'am, there is a young man in the cells. He was brought in with a bag full of cocaine in his possession.

He's got Delaney looking out for him. We're a couple of hours away. Don't let him walk before I get there."

The line was silent for several seconds. "Did you find Annie Alder?" Birch asked.

"Yes, ma'am. But I'm more concerned about this lad. He holds vital information. We've got two bodies, a growing drug problem, and youngsters wreaking havoc around the area. I must speak to him."

He heard the DCI sigh. "Okay, Calladine. I'll do what I can." She ended the call.

"I have no idea what's going on with Birch," he said to Ruth. "We can't make anything stick. Someone is doing everything they can to pull the rug from under this investigation."

CHAPTER 31

Calladine sat down opposite Andrew Harvey, Rocco at his side. "Right, Andrew, time to get serious." He and Ruth had made it back from Wales in record time and Calladine was keen to start the interview.

"Told him." The lad nodded in Rocco's direction, "I'm not saying owt."

"I'm afraid that's not how it works, lad. Talk to us and we'll help you. Persist with the attitude and you'll regret it."

Harvey looked at Delaney. "Is he threatening me?"

"No need," Calladine replied with a half-hearted smile. "Whoever is behind this will sort you out." He paused. Harvey looked puzzled. Time to enlighten him. "You got caught, Andrew," the DI explained patiently. "That wasn't in the plan. You lost the dope, worth a small fortune too. How d'you think the big boss feels about that?" He pursed his lips, shaking his head. "Bet he's angry, gunning for you probably. We let you go and your life won't be worth tuppence. Or perhaps that's not his plan. Perhaps he'll just let you rot in here. No one's come to help you get out so far, have they?"

Harvey nudged Delaney. "Is he right? I don't understand, why am I still here anyway? You said a couple of hours tops."

Delaney gave the detectives a smarmy smile. "May I have a private word with my client?"

"Ten minutes." Calladine and Rocco left the room.

"Have we got anything back on the knife?" Calladine asked when they were back in the incident room.

"I'll ring Julian."

"Can I have photos of Sean Barber and Frankie Halliwell?" Calladine asked Alice.

"How's it going?" Ruth asked.

"Reality is about to hit," Calladine said. "He's on his own, this one. No drugs, so I reckon the big boss doesn't want to know."

Calladine and Rocco resumed the interview.

"Feeling better now, Andrew?" Calladine asked.

The lad grunted a response. He didn't look happy.

"This isn't just about the drugs you were found with. It's a bit more serious than that. We're investigating two murders."

"I aint killed nobody," he fired back, his eyes wide with shock. "You can't pin that on me."

"I'm not saying you're responsible, Andrew, but you can help. Look at these photos and tell me if you know who any of these people are."

Calladine placed an image of Sean Barber in front of Harvey.

"I know him. That's Barber. Knifed on the street he was."

"Do you know who stabbed him?"

"No," Harvey said defensively. "But it wasn't me."

"Think carefully, Andrew. Help us and we'll help you."

"Someone said it was them men. You know, them going about sorting out the kids."

"It wasn't them though, was it?"

"Dean said Barber was a threat. Said days before Sean bought it that he wouldn't last long."

"A threat to what? The drug scam you had going?"

The lad scowled back. "Didn't ask what he meant."

"Dean who?"

"Dean Laycock."

"Are you and Dean friends?"

"Sometimes. We set things up together."

"What things?" asked Calladine.

The lad crossed his arms. "I've already said too much. My life is worth nowt if Street finds out."

"Ah, the elusive Street. The big boss, who'll likely have you killed the moment you step out of here. Great set-up the bloke's got, don't you think?"

Harvey looked at Calladine as if he'd just realised the reality of his situation.

"You know what we're talking about here," Calladine continued. "The temporary drug dens you set up in people's homes. People like Alex Geddes, for instance."

"Have you ever met Street, face to face?" Rocco asked.

"No, he texts. Reckons he's busy," Harvey replied.

"Do any of you have any theories about who he is? You must have talked about it amongst yourselves."

Harvey shrugged. "Never thought about it. The pay's okay and we have a laugh."

Calladine placed the photo of Frankie Halliwell on the table. "Know her?"

"Yeah. She came to one of the houses we'd taken over, looking for Sean."

This came as a surprise. "She knew Sean Barber?"

"Said so, didn't I."

"Did she find him?"

Harvey shook his head. "He weren't with us. She got angry and did one."

At that moment Alice came into the room, interrupting proceedings. She handed Calladine a note.

"I'll be back." He followed Alice to the incident room.

"The results have just come in, sir," she said. "Thought you should know at once." She handed him another sheet of paper.

"Prints found on the bag the knife was found in belong to Stokes," Calladine told the team. "We need to find him.

That man's stalking these crimes like a shadow. What about the knife itself?"

"Nothing found, apparently. He must have worn gloves."

"Gloves to do the stabbing, but not to wrap the weapon. Odd that."

"Are we doing anything about Annie and Billy?" Ruth asked. "Doing another runner is suspicious. I wouldn't mind talking to them again. Leaving that registration document like a cryptic clue for us to find? I'm sat here trying to work it out, but I'm stumped. And what's Giles Pennington got to do with anything?"

"Do we have his background now?"

"Yes, sir," replied Alice. "Before he turned up in Leesworth, Pennington worked for a firm in Sheffield. He was well thought of and they were sorry to see him go. He's not married and has no children. According to the woman I spoke to in Sheffield, he does have at least one failed relationship in the bag."

"Don't we all," Calladine remarked humourlessly. "Where does he live?"

"I haven't got an exact address, but he has an apartment in Bolton."

Calladine scratched his head. "Wonder how he met Alder? We need a word. Did he own that Audi and, if so, what was Sean Barber doing with it?"

Ruth picked up the phone. "I'm going to get onto the ports and airports — we don't want Annie and Billy skipping the country."

Calladine returned to the interview room.

"Can I go now?" Harvey asked.

"I'm afraid not, son. You'll be staying with us for a while yet."

The lad was indignant. "You can't keep me here. I've got places to be, things to do. This isn't fair."

"Does the name Conrad Stokes mean anything to you?" Calladine asked, ignoring this last remark.

"No." The boy was sullen.

"Any of your little gang mention the name?"

"No. No names. No grassing, that's our motto."

"You're still not getting it, are you, Andrew?" Calladine leaned forward across the desk. "You are in a lot of trouble. Help us and it could go easier for you."

"I know nowt."

"Where did the drugs come from?"

He shrugged. "Dunno."

"When you set up a den in someone's house, who delivers the stuff?"

"Some kids. Sometimes a few of them. Sometimes Barber did it."

"These kids, who were they? Did you know them?"

Another shrug. "Just kids. Young some of them, too. We'd bung 'em a tenner — they were happy with that."

"How young?" Calladine asked. "C'mon, Andrew, or we'll be here all night."

"I don't knock about with kids, so I can't tell you. They didn't say owt, just dropped off the gear and did one."

"The Hobfield is a small estate, are you sure you didn't recognise anyone?"

"I've told you, no."

"My colleague was attacked by one of your gang — Dean Laycock. Another lad made off with a holdall, wouldn't give it up when told to. Drugs?"

Andrew Harvey nodded.

"What's his name?"

"I don't know. He's not local. Look, I've said too much. They'll kill me for this."

"Nothing to lose by telling me in that case, Andrew." The lad ran a hand down his face. "Tyler Dodd."

Not a name Calladine knew. "Not local, so where's he from?"

"Other side of Manchester."

"I want you to look at some photos, Andrew. While I get them sorted, I want you to write down the names of everyone else in your little gang. I'll be back later." He turned to the uniformed officer standing in the corner. "Once he's finished writing, take him back to the cells."

"How'd it go?" Ruth asked as Calladine entered the incident room.

"Andrew Harvey knows a little. It was young kids who delivered the drugs. Bring Dean Laycock in again. Tell him we're holding his mate and let's see if that makes him any more talkative. Also, ask the Manchester force if they have anything on a Tyler Dodd. We need a word with him too."

"I'll do that," Rocco said.

Ruth yawned. "Well, I'm off home. Jake and Harry to see to. After leaving them to their own devices for a couple of days, God knows what sort of a state the house'll be in."

Calladine said goodnight then turned to Alice. "Get me photos of Richard Alder, Giles Pennington and Billy Alder. Let's see if Andrew Harvey recognises any of them."

"Richard and Billy Alder are on the incident board, sir," the DC replied. "Hopefully there's one of Pennington on the Sheffield company's website."

"Okay. In the meantime, I'm off to have another word with Alf Alder. See if Billy's been in touch."

* * *

Alf Alder wasn't pleased to see Calladine. He opened the door and swore. "Just leave me alone. Them kids have given me hell since you were here last."

Calladine was used to such cold welcomes on the Hobfield. Many of the estate's residents distrusted the police and were often uncooperative. He wanted to prove to Alf that he could help.

"In what way, Alf?" he asked.

"Caterwauling around the deck. Name calling. God knows why. One knocked on the door asking for Billy. Wouldn't 'ave it that he weren't 'ere. No idea what he wanted."

"Has Billy been in touch?"

"Not a word. Mind you, that's normal for him. Goes missing for days on end. He'll come home when he's good and ready."

"If he does contact you, please phone me at once. You have my card. These kids who were bothering you, d'you have any names?"

"No idea. Probably that football lot," he said, coughing. "Told them I'd have a word with their parents, not that I know them. That did it, though, flew down that deck like rats up a ginnel."

Calladine was puzzled. Why should Alf Alder be of such interest to those kids? More questions for Andrew Harvey and Dean Laycock.

CHAPTER 32

Day 8

Ruth had phoned in early to say she'd be late. She was having the dressing on her hand seen to. Calladine was at his desk reading through the reports of sightings of Billy and Annie that had come in overnight. There was only one that held promise. They'd allegedly been spotted in a Carmarthenshire village called Llangunnor. Like Ynyslas, it was sparsely populated. The problem he had was there were another dozen reports just like that one, and all different locations.

"I'll have another go at Andrew Harvey this morning. Do we have the photos?" he asked Alice.

"Pennington is posing a problem, sir," she replied. "He doesn't appear anywhere on his former employer's website and he has no social media presence either."

"I'm going to Alder's factory soon. If necessary, I'll take one myself," Calladine decided. "Speak to this company in Sheffield, see if they've got one in their records they can email over."

"DI Calladine, can I have a word?" It was DCI Birch, and for the first time this week, she'd asked, not barked.

"Of course, ma'am."

"We'll go to the canteen," she said. "I could do with something to eat."

It was unusual for her to invite anyone to join her. "Everything okay, ma'am?" he asked as they headed down the stairs.

"Not really."

"Do you want to discuss it?"

"No. But I have no choice, as it concerns you."

Intrigued, Calladine followed her to a table in the far corner of the canteen. While he waited, she went to the counter and returned with two coffees. "When I saw the food, I couldn't face it. That's what worry does to you." She gave him a half-hearted smile. "Did you find the Alder woman and Billy?"

"Yes, ma'am, and we spoke to them. However, they appear to have moved on since. Annie Alder is terrified of her husband and what he might do if he catches up with her." Calladine shook his head. "We may have to bring them in now. Billy Alder is certainly of interest. We found the registration document for the burnt-out Audi in his rubbish bin. That's a conversation in itself." Now for the tricky bit. "We're still looking for this 'Street' character. We have no choice. He's a big part of what's going on."

Birch gave him a hard look before speaking. "I suspect that DCS Chesworth is in the pay of whoever is orchestrating these crimes. I suspect that his brief is to make anything that might out this 'Street' person go away. I also suspect that he has been turning a blind eye to a lot of other misdemeanours recently. How the current drug problem is related, I don't know. Those vulnerable residents you reported on, at least one report has 'disappeared.' The Rowena Hargreaves one. I wanted to check the details and looked for it on the system — nothing."

Calladine was stunned. Coming from Birch, this was a serious allegation. "Bill Geddes will not drop it until someone is facing charges, and one of my officers was injured during the Hopkins bust. Even Chesworth can't make that go away."

"Not yet he can't, but over time, who knows?"

"If what you suspect is true, then Chesworth is getting paid by a criminal gang to help them."

"I realise that. But the problem with Chesworth has only come to light during this case. I'm not sure why or how he was got at. But I do know that he and this 'Street' person must have a connection."

"It could be blackmail, ma'am. Perhaps something dodgy in Chesworth's past."

"I don't know, but Chesworth is up to his neck in it. There is no proof as yet, but as the senior investigating officer you must tread carefully. Do you understand, Calladine? Your career depends on it," she warned.

"There's a lot of drug dealing going on in the town. I have no idea who is implicated as yet. Pennington is in the frame, and we can't rule him out for the murder of Frankie Halliwell, despite having no proof."

"In what way is Pennington implicated?"

"The blade that killed Frankie was found taped under the seat of Pennington's burnt-out car. A car being used by one of the drug crew, Sean Barber."

"Where did you find the car?"

"The Hobfield."

"In that case, anyone could have planted the knife there. Any reasonable solicitor would soon get round that one. Anything else?"

"Not yet, ma'am, but I plan to see both Alder and Pennington this morning. I will have to tell Alder that we've found his wife and that his daughter is safe."

"If I'm right, he'll already know. The report you filed — DCS Chesworth will have seen it. I don't like any of this. But I need something concrete before I take my suspicions to the anti-corruption unit. At which time they will either throw me out on my ear or this mess will be investigated at last."

"I'm sure they'll take you seriously, ma'am." He smiled.

"Don't bank on it. Isaac Chesworth has some powerful friends."

A sobering thought. Calladine checked his watch. "I'd better get on with it then. Once I've spoken to Alder and Pennington, I'll report back."

* * *

Calladine took Alice with him to Alder's office. The place was as busy as ever. Lorries queued at the gates waiting to get in. The factory must be working at full capacity.

"It's some business he's built here," Alice remarked, looking around. "Look at that lorry — from the sign on its side, it's come all the way across Europe."

"Ingredients for the biscuits, I imagine. They have some turnover. Most of the UK supermarkets take their stuff, and they export, too," Calladine told her. "Come on, let's get this sorted."

They found Richard Alder and Giles Pennington together in Alder's office. Pennington's face was thunderous. The pair had been arguing again.

"I'll leave you to it," Pennington said. "I just popped in to invite Richard to lunch." He turned to Alder. "I'll wait in reception."

"We will require a word with you before we go," Calladine said. "Don't leave the building."

"That sounds like a threat, Inspector. What the hell do you imagine I've done?"

"I'm not sure, but I've got a growing list of possibilities." Pennington's face turned a deep red as he disappeared through the door.

"Arrested my wife yet?" Alder blasted, once Pennington had left. "Surely she can't evade the law for ever? Your DCI Birch told me that Sophie is safe, so effectively, Annie has kidnapped my daughter. I insist that Sophie is returned to me at once. Annie is unfit to be anyone's mother, never mind a three-year-old child."

"We have spoken to her," Calladine confirmed. "Your daughter is fine. In good health and quite happy."

Alder slammed his fist on the desk top. "I want her back! Do your job and stop making excuses!"

"Did you know that Annie's sister, Frankie, has been killed?"

Alder's head shot up and he stared at the pair. "No one said anything to me. Why wasn't I told? How did it happen?"

He appeared genuinely shocked and that surprised Calladine. "She was stabbed, Mr Alder. Murdered."

Alder poured himself a whiskey. All the puff had gone from his sails. "Frankie was a loose cannon, and loud, but she was harmless. Who'd want her dead?"

"That's what we're trying to find out. When did you see her last?"

"I can't remember. What with all the palaver around Annie's disappearance, I've had only one thing on my mind — Sophie."

"It would help our investigation if you could remember, Mr Alder. We are trying to re-trace her last movements."

"She wasn't staying at the house anymore. I can't face it either, now that Annie and Sophie aren't there."

Alice spoke. "Annie is afraid of you Mr Alder — did you know that? She's afraid that if she returns you will do her harm."

"What? Why? I've never done anything to hurt her. And I've certainly never threatened her."

"We found her living in an isolated spot," Calladine said. "She said it was so that you wouldn't find her. She gave us the impression that if you did, their lives were at risk."

"She's lying! I don't know why, but she knows I'd never hurt her. Why is she doing this?" His face hardened. "What is going on inside that head of hers? Annie is my world. I thought we had it all." He shook his head. "You must have got it wrong. My Annie knows me well enough to know I'm not a violent man. I lose it now and again, but not with her. Usually it's about the business. It's a huge responsibility."

"She was very frightened, so much so that she didn't trust us to keep her whereabouts from you. Annie has moved on again, and the search is ongoing."

"I don't know what's going on. She plotted and schemed to rip me off and steal our child, but even now I don't hate her. I want them back. We need to put Sophie first and begin again."

Calladine could see that Alder was struggling to get his head around this revelation. "How long have you known Mr Pennington?"

Alder looked up. "I met Giles about a year ago at the country club I go to. He's a useful man to know. He's very experienced in the import and export field."

Alice nodded. "We saw the lorries outside. Your brother, Billy, worked as transport manager?"

"He's my brother, I can't not employ him." He raised an eyebrow at her. "Not that he was up to much. Took too much time off." Alder looked at Calladine and his expression hardened. "I heard that he's with Annie. Is that true?"

"Yes, they're together."

"Is he why she left me? Does she love him?"

"I've no idea, but they seemed close."

"I don't know why she told you all that rubbish about me, but I bet it has a lot to do with Billy. I intend to get my daughter back. If Annie wants to come home, I won't say no. When you find her, tell her that I want them back, both of them."

Calladine was about to reply when his mobile rang. It was Ruth. He excused himself and went out into the corridor.

"I've got something interesting for you," she began. "We have a photo from the firm in Sheffield who employed Giles Pennington. I've texted you. Take a look."

Calladine accessed the text. The image he was looking at was not the man Alder had befriended.

CHAPTER 33

Calladine passed the phone to Alice to take a look. "Thank you for your time, Mr Alder. We may have more questions at a later date." He stood in the doorway. "We'll have a word with Mr Pennington before we leave."

"Please find them," Alder implored. "Like I said, I want Sophie back. I'm her father and have every right. Tell Annie I forgive her and to just come home."

Outside in the corridor, Alice handed the phone back to Calladine. "What's going on? Alder is upset, he didn't put that on. That was a genuine show of emotion in there. The man is cut to shreds about Annie and what she's done to him. Even so, he still wants her back! What d'you think, sir?"

"I don't know, but I'll find out. Someone's doing a good job at pulling the wool over our eyes. At the moment I can't work it out. But Annie and Billy ran for a reason. That much is certain."

They found 'Pennington' sitting on a sofa in a corner of reception.

"If the man sat there isn't Pennington, then who is he?" Alice whispered as they approached.

"Let's find out. I'll have a word first, get the measure of the man. Meanwhile, can you radio the station for backup.

We might need to take Pennington — or whoever he is — in, and he could put up a fight."

Calladine sat down opposite Pennington. He looked nervous. His eyes watched Alice as she made the call outside.

"So how can I help?" he asked amiably.

"You can tell me who you really are for starters," Calladine began. "Because we know you're not Giles Pennington."

The man heaved a deep sigh and sat back on the sofa. "Okay, you've found me out. Big deal."

"It might be," Calladine said. "We have a few questions to ask you regarding the deaths of Sean Barber and Frankie Halliwell."

"That's a hell of a leap, Inspector! I'm living under an assumed identity, therefore I'm a killer! Not me, no way!" His face had turned a shade of purple. "I didn't kill anyone. You've got this all wrong."

"We'll be the judge of that. Meanwhile, do you mind telling me who you really are?"

"And if I refuse to say?"

"Then I'll arrest you, because you've obviously got something to hide." Calladine smiled. "You can speak to me here or down at the station. Your choice."

"Okay, I'll come with you. But I want my solicitor present, and it's on the understanding that you don't alert Alder or anyone else round here. Once we've got this little mess sorted, I still have to live here."

"We can't promise anything. You're not local, anyway — don't you live Bolton way?"

"I'm planning a move to a house in Hopecross." Pennington picked up his coat and accompanied Calladine across the car park to the waiting police car. The inspector glanced up at the office block. Richard Alder was watching them.

* * *

"Look, nothing but a small plaster," Ruth held up her injured hand. "I can drive now."

175

Calladine smiled. "Good. What's the latest on Annie and Billy?"

"They've been sighted all over the country. But the Carmarthen one is by far the most promising."

Pity. Calladine didn't fancy chasing off down there. "We've brought Pennington in. He's being processed now. Any idea who he is?"

"I have a theory, but we'll need his fingerprint results to prove it."

"You're thinking Conrad Stokes?"

Ruth nodded.

"Me too, although we haven't had that conversation yet. Stokes was an infamous Glasgow villain, or he was two decades ago. He went down for several offences, not least grievous bodily harm."

"Doesn't look the type, does he?" Alice said. "He was no trouble coming in. Just sat in the back of the car, quiet as you please."

"Don't be taken in," Calladine warned. "If that man is Stokes, then he's dangerous."

"We need more against Stokes than some prints on a plastic bag," Ruth reminded him. "Forensics found nothing on the blade, and that registration document doesn't prove anything."

"I'll have another word with Andrew Harvey first, see if he recognises Pennington's photo."

Calladine went to speak to Birch in her office. "It turns out Giles Pennington isn't who he says he is, ma'am. His fingerprints should reveal who he really is, but I suspect he'll turn out to be Stokes."

"Even if he does, we don't have enough evidence against him," she said. "Nothing concrete that links him to the killings. What about Richard Alder?"

"I still can't make my mind up about him. My instincts tell me he's okay. What you see is what you get. He wants his daughter back, he's angry with his wife, but he insists that he didn't threaten anyone. He was astonished when I told him that Annie was afraid of him."

Birch looked at him. "Annie Alder tried very hard to convince you otherwise. Who do you believe? A frightened woman who hightailed it off to some remote part of Wales for safety, or her husband, who's lost his child, his wife to his brother, and therefore his self-respect?"

"I don't know who to believe, ma'am. But Alder does want his child back and that's only natural."

"There is a lot about this case we still don't understand. Rule Pennington in or out, then find Annie and Billy and bring them in. If, as you say, your instinct falls in favour of the husband, why are they running? Is it because they're afraid or something else?"

* * *

"Can I go home now?" Andrew Harvey asked Calladine the minute he set foot in the interview room. "My mum's not much cop, but even she'll be worried sick by now."

"She's been told," Calladine nodded. "She's not happy, but understands the score."

"What now? I've told you everything I know."

"Not quite. Do you know this man?" He placed a photo of Giles Pennington on the table.

"No. Who is he?"

"Never mind that, are you sure you've never seen him?"

"Said so, didn't I. He looks like some posh bloke. We never bothered anyone like him."

Time at the nick had worn the lad down. All the high-handed bluster had gone. He was on his own and he knew it. Calladine's gut told him Harvey was telling the truth.

"Okay, Andrew. I'll see if we can get you bailed." Calladine left the room.

"Andrew Harvey didn't recognise Pennington," he told the team back in the incident room.

"Well, I've got some good news," Ruth smiled. "Pennington is definitely Stokes. Fingerprints are on file and they match."

Calladine studied the incident board. They had the murders of Sean Barber and Frankie Halliwell, and a drugs scam involving what seemed like half the town. "Where are they getting the drugs from?" he voiced the question out loud. "That was a sizeable amount we found on Harvey. What had been cut and dealt in the properties looked sizable too. Whoever this Street is, he has some contacts."

"Given Stokes's background, perhaps he can help with that one," Ruth suggested sarcastically.

"We'll see. Any luck finding this Tyler Dodd?" Calladine asked.

"The Manchester force have sent uniforms to his last known address. If they find him, he's ours," Rocco said.

"And you'll be able to recognise him from the night you were attacked?" Calladine asked Ruth.

"Yes. He was the one who legged it with the holdall."

"Andrew Harvey will be bailed. If he gets involved with the gang again, we'll haul him back and keep him in the cells."

CHAPTER 34

'Giles Pennington,' or whoever he really was, appeared relaxed as he waited to be interviewed with his solicitor. Calladine was surprised that it wasn't Delaney.

"Will this take long, Inspector?" he asked Calladine as he and Ruth entered the room. "You know my situation. I'd like to return and explain to Richard what's happened."

"You will be with us for some time. We have the fingerprint results back," Calladine faced him. "You're Conrad Stokes."

He looked at Robert Crawford, his solicitor. "I don't wish to comment on that."

"You heard my client," Crawford's replied.

"Fingerprints don't lie, so it's pointless denying it. Does Richard Alder know your true identity?"

"Yes, he does."

"I find that difficult to believe. Why would he befriend a man with your reputation? You are a thug and a drug dealer," Calladine said.

Pennington's eyes narrowed. He didn't like that. "Why am I here? I have done nothing wrong. Granted, I have a past. I hold my hands up to that. But I'm not that man anymore."

"Did you own a black Audi?"

"No, but I had use of one," he admitted. "From the Alder's fleet. I borrowed it for several weeks prior to buying one of my own. After which, I returned it."

"You took it back to Alder's?"

Pennington nodded.

"So you'll be surprised to learn that we found the Audi burnt out on the Hobfield. We suspect it was being used by a gang who were distributing drugs around the town."

Pennington shook his head. "Drugs! So naturally, you drag me in." It was obvious to Calladine that he was seething. "I am not responsible. Whatever's going on around here has nothing to do with me."

"A murder weapon was found hidden in that car."

Pennington stared at Calladine. "I repeat, nothing to do with me. You have the wrong man. I'm not dealing drugs and I didn't murder anyone."

"Not recently," Calladine smiled.

"I now have a new identity and I'm building a new future."

"Mr . . ." Calladine smiled at the man. "Which do you prefer, Pennington or Stokes?"

"I'm Giles Pennington now." The reply was firm.

"Giles Pennington worked for a firm in Sheffield and looks nothing like you. Isn't that identity theft?" Ruth said.

"Giles is dead, so he'll hardly complain."

Calladine leaned forward. "You were having a relationship with Frankie Halliwell. She was murdered, and with the same weapon we found in your car." He paused, giving the man time to take this in. "So you see my problem."

Pennington inhaled. "I admit that I did have a fling with Frankie. But she was too full-on. She wanted a relationship. Frankie's sister had just got married and she wanted the same. That isn't for me, I'm afraid."

"Did you tell her this?"

Pennington nodded.

"Having met Frankie, I'll bet that didn't go down too well. Volatile young woman. Loses it when she's angry. Take it badly, did she?"

"For a while, but then she found someone else to lavish her attentions on. I was soon forgotten."

"Did she tell you about the baby?"

Pennington looked shocked. He obviously had no idea.

Calladine continued. "Frankie was pregnant at the time of her murder. Tests carried out showed that you were the father."

Pennington covered his face with his hands. "I didn't know. She should have told me."

"What would you have done? You've just admitted you didn't want a relationship."

"We'd have worked something out. I would have provided for them both. Look, you've got this wrong, I didn't kill her or anyone else."

Calladine shook his head. "The problem is, Mr Pennington, I don't believe you. We have your car, the weapon, and very soon we'll have proof that links you to the drug dealing that's gone on round here recently. A warrant is being organised to search your home, your phone records, and your bank accounts. We'll find what we're looking for, and you will be charged."

"No need for a warrant, Inspector. Go ahead and look at whatever you please."

* * *

"I'm not sure about him," Ruth said as they walked back to the incident room. "He comes across as genuine, and he's happy for us to rummage around in his life."

"He's a crook. Have you read the report we received from Glasgow? Pennington, Stokes — whatever name he's using — is a villain of the first order. Don't be taken in. He was perfectly placed to carry out the murders *and* organise the drug deals."

"You think he's 'Street?'"

"Yes, I do. But I'm leaving that conversation for later. I want the results of the searches first."

They reached the incident room. "Rocco, have we got those warrants yet?" Calladine asked.

"We don't need them," Ruth reminded him. "Pennington gave us permission."

"I'm not taking any chances," he told her. "I don't want any comebacks when we find something."

"They've just come through, sir," Rocco confirmed. "Where do you want to start?"

"Me and Ruth will look at his home. You and Alice go through his phone and bank records. Cross-check against any phone numbers we're already looking at, particularly those belonging to Street and his gang." He turned to Ruth. "Come on, let's get this done with."

Calladine wasn't happy. Ruth had voiced her doubts about Pennington and if he was honest, he wasn't so sure himself. What was missing was solid evidence. The Audi belonged to Alder's company. As for the registration document, that was still a puzzle. The plastic bag in which the knife was wrapped could have been deliberately placed. Birch was right, any lawyer worth his salt would have him released in no time. The CPS were unlikely to go with what they had either.

Ruth interrupted his thoughts. "Bolton is a bit of a ride out."

"Too bad, we have no choice. It's clutching at straws time, Ruth. We've been working on this for days and still got very little."

"We've found Sophie Alder. That's put a lot of people's minds at ease, not least of all mine. I hate missing kids cases."

* * *

They drove down the motorway and half an hour later Calladine pulled up in the car park outside Stokes' two-storey apartment block. The well-manicured gardens offered views out towards the surrounding hills. "How much, d'you reckon?" he asked Ruth.

"Not cheap," she answered. "Nothing is round here. But does he rent or has he bought?"

"Phone Rocco, get him to find out."

A van full of uniformed officers was waiting for them. "The solicitor gave me the key, sir." One of them handed it to Calladine. "Asked if we'd keep the place tidy."

"We'll do our best."

Leaving Ruth on her mobile to Rocco, Calladine went inside. The place was immaculate. The décor was understated but expensive. Calladine made straight for a desk by the window and sat down. He picked up the laptop and handed it to one of the uniforms. "Get this looked at by the techies." He opened the drawers but found nothing of interest.

"Tom," said Ruth, entering the room. "Rocco has got something. Pennington owns this place outright, but not only that, he lent Alder the ransom money."

Calladine was astonished. "Are you sure? That's a huge amount."

"Well, a transfer of one million was made to Richard Alder from Pennington's account in readiness. There was a sizeable balance left too."

"Where did he get that sort of money from? Surely the proceeds of his previous criminal activity would have been confiscated?"

"We'll have to ask him. But what's the betting it's the proceeds of more recent crimes. His recent drug dealing, for example? There is something else, and this might cheer you up." She smiled. "Pennington's phone records are in. Alice found both Sean Barber's and Dean Laycock's numbers amongst them."

Calladine smiled. It looked as if they'd got him. Those lads had no legitimate connection to Pennington that he was aware of.

"I'm going back to the station. I want to speak to him again. Let's see him wriggle out of this."

"I'll carry on with the search," said Ruth. "The sniffer dogs are due any minute. If Pennington has had drugs here, we'll know soon enough. I'll get a lift back with one of the uniforms."

They were making progress and Calladine felt a great deal happier on the drive back. Pennington was a cool character, but he'd be hard-pressed to talk his way round the new evidence.

* * *

Rocco handed Calladine several sheets of paper. "I've highlighted the calls and labelled them — Barber, Laycock and Street."

"Street rang Pennington? Shame. I had him down as being our elusive villain. So much for that theory." Calladine scanned down the list. He frowned. "These are all incoming calls. Pennington didn't phone any of them, and each call was only a few seconds long. That doesn't make sense. I would have expected more calls and for longer. This is some operation they've got going. It takes organising. That requires longer than a few seconds."

"Call-wise, it's all we've got," said Rocco. "But don't forget the money. It's a large amount — where did he get it from?"

"Good question," said Calladine. "I'll go and ask him."

CHAPTER 35

"I think I've been here long enough, Inspector." Pennington greeted Calladine with a cold look. "I've answered all your questions. You've had access to my home and my finances. I've been candid, there's nothing I can add."

Calladine sat down opposite Pennington and his solicitor and placed the phone records on the table in front of him. "There are a couple of things I'd like to clear up first," he said. "The money you used to buy your apartment and lend to Alder to pay the ransom, where did it come from?"

Pennington's face was expressionless. "I'll remind you that the ransom was never paid, so I'll get that money back. If it had been paid over, I wouldn't have minded. It is my intention to buy into the Alder factory. That money would have been payment for shares. Once the dust has settled, I'm hopeful the deal will still go through."

"Nonetheless, you had it to lend."

"Do you know anything about my background, Inspector?"

"I know you're a villain from Glasgow, that you've been inside for large-scale drug dealing."

"I'm talking about my family background."

"Is that relevant?"

"I didn't simply pluck the name Giles Pennington out of thin air. Giles was a cousin on my mother's side. They came from Sheffield. The firm where he worked was owned by my mother's family, and I was a shareholder. Both my parents are dead, as are Giles's, and I have no siblings. I inherited the lot, plus a large estate belonging to my mother." He paused. "I suggest you take a little time to check it out and then I expect to be released."

Calladine jotted down some notes and handed them to a PC, asking him to hand them to Ruth in the incident room. "These are your mobile phone records." He indicated the sheets of paper on the desk. "We have interviewed a number of the kids being used to distribute the drugs. Can you explain what their numbers are doing on your phone?"

"Frankly, no. I do not mix with 'kids,' as you put it. There must be some mistake."

"Did my client make these calls, Inspector?" Crawford asked.

"No. They were incoming from persons of interest in this case."

"As I'm sure you're aware, that proves nothing. They phoned him, perhaps by accident, perhaps to set him up. I think Mr Pennington has been here for long enough. If there is nothing else, we're leaving."

He was right. Calladine had nothing. He was still woefully short of the proof he needed to charge Pennington.

* * *

Later that day Calladine called the team together for a briefing.

"We found nothing in Pennington's apartment. The place doesn't look as if anyone lives there," Ruth told the team.

Rocco spoke up. "His bank records are interesting. I checked on the money." He gave a whistle. "He wasn't lying. The guy inherited over two million. Bailing out Alder wasn't an issue for him. But I still don't understand why he'd do it."

"He's after a share in the company," Calladine replied. "Any sign of drugs?" Calladine asked Ruth.

She shook her head. "The place is clean. He's clean. He's either very clever or he has nothing to do with this."

Calladine turned to Alice. "How are the Manchester force doing with finding Dodd?"

"They've been to his home, sir. He sometimes lives with an older brother in a flat in Hulme. He hasn't seen him for a few days. He says this is normal, and that his brother travels around a lot."

"Well, he would, he's the delivery boy, isn't he," Rocco scoffed. "Does he have a car?"

"No. According to his brother, Tyler uses public transport," Alice replied.

"Less chance of being traced. Got it all wrapped up, haven't they?" Rocco shook his head.

"Are we working on the premise that Dodd is 'Street?'" Ruth asked.

"He could be." Calladine was thoughtful. "But there has to be someone else at the top of this chain. The youngsters deliver to various addresses. A tenner a time, Harvey told us. Tyler Dodd delivers the supply to whichever area he's told to. It's whoever is supplying *him* we have to get our hands on. He's the man at the top."

"We don't even have anyone in the frame," Ruth pointed out. "Pennington seemed possible, but not now. We can't find any evidence against him."

Calladine stared at the incident board. It was an array of faces, names, and dates. It all added up to a big fat nothing. Someone had killed Sean Barber and Frankie Halliwell, but who or why was still a mystery.

"Okay, we'll call it a day. Thinking caps on, folks. See if you can come up with a new angle to investigate."

"Want to come to mine to eat?" Ruth offered as they packed up. "Can't promise much, but at least you won't be on your own."

Calladine was grateful for the offer, but he wasn't much in the mood for company. The case was running rings round them and he wanted to collect his thoughts. "I'm alright," he smiled. "You get off and don't mind me."

Ruth grabbed her coat and left him to it. Heaving a sigh, Calladine sat down at his desk to look through the case file yet again.

"Calladine." It was DCI Birch. "I think we should talk," she said. "I suggest we decamp to the pub across the road. Get some food and down a couple of drinks."

This was unusual. Calladine was curious. "Good idea, ma'am. I was only going home to walk the dog anyway."

* * *

"I've applied for a transfer," Birch announced once they were sitting down. "I was considering it anyway, but all this trouble with DCS Chesworth has swung it. The man is heading for a fall and I won't be dragged down with him."

Calladine was shocked. He didn't know what he'd been expecting, but it wasn't that. He wasn't overly fond of Rhona Birch, but she was a known quantity. If she went, they could get anyone as the new DCI.

"I have already started the process," she continued. "With Long being laid up, your name has been thrown into the pot as acting DCI. Do a good job, make the application, and it could be permanent."

He was surprised. His past was far from unblemished. For starters, he'd been dogged by his association with Ray Fallon for most of his career. Fallon had been one of Manchester's most notorious gangsters — and Calladine's cousin. Granted, Fallon was dead now, but there were those who had wondered where his loyalties lay.

"I've always been overlooked before," he reminded her.

"Yes, and I know why." She appeared to read his thoughts. "But Fallon's not around anymore, and apart from your association with him, you have an excellent record." She paused and took a slug of her wine. "It would help your cause if you got this case sorted, and the quicker the better. Two murders, and the drug dealing. Throw in apprehending a big-time dealer and I think we can safely say the post is yours. I will of course put in a good word for you."

"Thank you, ma'am. Very kind."

"Not really. I want to finish my stint in Leesworth on a high. It'll stand me in good stead in my next position."

"Dare I ask where and what that is?"

"No, Calladine. Until I'm sure, it's strictly my business only."

CHAPTER 36

After his interesting conversation with Birch, Calladine walked home. He'd had a couple of pints and wouldn't risk driving. He was more cheerful than he'd been in a while. The idea of being DCI appealed to him, and given the years he'd worked at Leesdon station as a DI, he deserved it. Having arrived home, he was just about to wander round the block with Sam when his mobile rang.

"Them damn kids keep banging on my door, shouting for our Billy. They've been at it for hours. Nothing I say will shift them. I'm at my wits end. I can't get any peace."

Alf Alder sounded upset. He was an old man, and Calladine felt he had little choice but to go round, see what was going on. He'd take Sam with him. Kill two birds with one stone.

The Hobfield was dark and uninviting at night. The tower blocks loomed over the area, tall and poorly lit. Calladine got out of his car and stood in the concrete square staring up at the block of flats. Over the years he'd investigated many crimes committed here. He shuddered and pulled his collar up — the estate was no place to linger.

Alf was in a state when Calladine arrived at his flat in Heron House. "They won't listen. Our Billy isn't here. But still they ring the bell and scream for him. I'm sorry to bother you, but you did give me this." He waved Calladine's card in his face.

"It's okay, Alf. D'you know who these kids are?"

"I presume they're his football lads. He coaches the team off the estate a couple of times a week. One were Laycock's younger brother, Kane. Right little tearaway he is."

"Well, they've gone now, Alf. There's not much I can do."

"Will you find them and have a word, Mr Calladine? Tell them to lay off."

Calladine frowned. "Laycock, you say? I know Dean. His lot live a few floors up. I'll go and have a word. I'll leave Sam with you if that's okay, pick him up in a bit."

Alf looked at Sam. "He's a funny-looking dog. Is he supposed to be that wrinkly?"

Calladine laughed. Sam wasn't the most handsome of dogs. "Yes, Alf, it's the breed. Sam's a Shar Pei."

Calladine left Sam with Alf and went in search of the younger Laycock boy. Their flat was on the sixth floor. He was met by four young lads chasing up and down the deck.

"I'm looking for Kane Laycock," he called to them.

"You police?"

"Yes son, so don't give me any lip."

"That's their flat there," he pointed. "Dean's not well. Kane's had to go back in and see to him."

The front door was ajar. Calladine peered into the darkness and called out, "Anyone here?"

A young lad, no more than twelve, came running to greet him. "It's our Dean, he's not right." Grabbing his arm, the lad pulled Calladine into the flat.

"Your parents not here?"

"Me mum hasn't been home in a while," the kid admitted. "And me dad's long gone."

Taking a closer look, Calladine could see that the boy's clothes were dirty and the flat was a pigsty. Dean Laycock lay on an old sofa, unconscious.

There were several small clear plastic bags lying on a coffee table beside him. It was obvious that he'd overdosed.

Calladine was on his mobile for an ambulance. Then, "How long's he been like this?" he asked Kane.

The lad shrugged. "I don't know. I've been out with me mates."

Calladine knelt down beside Dean. He was barely breathing. "C'mon lad, wake up." He slapped his cheeks, trying to bring him round. With one ear pressed to Dean's chest, he could barely hear a heartbeat. There was no time to lose: Calladine started chest compressions.

"He asked me to find Billy, but he's not around. He got upset, kept going on about wanting out. Then some mate he knows came round and got angry. He hit our Dean and said he'd be back. Dean told him he wanted to stop, but his mate wouldn't have it. He gave Dean some of that stuff," he nodded at the coffee table. "He's an addict." He lowered his head. "Dean didn't want to, but his mate said it would sort everything."

Re-checking Dean's chest, the heartbeat was stronger. Calladine rang the station. He wanted a couple of uniforms to keep an eye on the place. He glanced at the plastic bags on the coffee table beside Dean. If he'd taken that lot, he'd be lucky to survive. He'd get a CSI team round, too.

"He got off his head because he's in big trouble," Kane said. "That mate of his said he'd let the big boss down."

"Do you know this boss?"

"No, but I think he's called Street."

Calladine took hold of the boy by the shoulders. "Has he ever been here, this Street?"

"I don't think so."

"This mate who came tonight, can you describe him? It's very important. He hurt your brother. We need to find him before he hurts anyone else."

The lad looked worried. "I'll be in trouble if I do. The boss, Street, won't like it. He isn't someone you mess with — look at him." He nodded at Dean.

"You're okay, Kane. I'll make sure you're safe. Have you any idea where your mother might be?"

He shook his head. "She goes off for days on end. I haven't seen her all this week."

"Do you have any other family nearby?"

"Me gran. She lives in the old folk's bungalows near the green."

"Will she let you stay?"

Kane nodded.

"Okay. Now don't worry. I'll get Dean to hospital and arrange for one of my officers to take you to your gran's."

Calladine had no idea how old his grandmother was, but it was unlikely Kane staying with her would become a permanent arrangement as she was in her seventies and living in one-bedroomed accommodation. If his mother didn't show up and claim him, Kane Laycock would likely end up in care. But he wouldn't labour the point yet.

Seconds later the ambulance arrived. One of the two paramedics was Layla. She gave him a cursory nod.

"His name is Dean Laycock. He's overdosed on something," Calladine said. "He doesn't look good. His heart is weak and his breathing shallow."

The pair started to work on Dean. Calladine moved the coffee table out of the way. He wanted to preserve the evidence. "Does Dean have a mobile?" he asked Kane.

The lad was staring wide eyed as Layla attached a drip to Dean's arm. He was shaking, obviously scared.

"It's okay," Calladine said. "They know what they're doing."

"Do we take him in too?" Layla asked.

"No. I'll get an officer to take him to his gran's for the night." Calladine had spotted a mobile on the carpet by the sofa, probably where Dean had dropped it. "This his?" he asked Kane.

The lad nodded. "Think so. He has different ones all the time."

Calladine bagged it and went to look for the uniforms he'd requested.

"He's in a bad way," Layla whispered to him as they stretchered Dean out of the small flat. "Just as well you found him when you did. I'm no expert, but this doesn't look like an ordinary overdose to me."

Calladine's head snapped up. "What d'you mean?"

"Get the residue in those packets checked, but I suspect you'll find it's been cut with something else."

Calladine turned to Kane, who was now cowering in a corner of the room. "Don't worry, son. I'll make sure you're okay." He smiled. "This mate who came to see Dean, d'you know what they were arguing about?"

"Our Dean was supposed to give him something, but he didn't have it. He said his contact had disappeared. His mate got angry. Said Dean had better sort it or else."

Calladine had no way of knowing what this 'something' was, but he suspected it was drugs. Dean Laycock's place was a pick-up point. But who was supplying him?

* * *

It was a couple of hours before Calladine picked up Sam from Alf Alder's. The dog was happily curled up in front of his gas fire.

Alf was smiling. "He's good company, and he guards the place well. It's made me think, way things are around here, might get one of my own."

"He needs a lot of walking, Alf. Think carefully before doing anything rash. Those kids have settled now. The Laycocks had a visitor, left Dean in a bad way. Did you see or hear anything earlier?"

"No, just them kids shouting for Billy."

"D'you know why they wanted him?"

"Summat to do with the football team, I expect. I don't hear so well. It was just so much noise."

"Okay, Alf. I've left an officer upstairs keeping an eye out. Any more trouble, give him a shout."

CHAPTER 37

Day 9

"Dean Laycock is in hospital. He overdosed last night," Calladine told the team at the briefing the following morning. "Whatever he took had been cut with something toxic. We'll find out soon enough. Forensics will have analysed it by now. And I have this." He held up the evidence bag containing the mobile he'd retrieved. "No doubt a disposable. His brother told me he gets through them."

"You should have rung me," Ruth frowned. "I could have helped."

"No time, and I didn't expect it to be more than giving a few kids an earful. I got a call from Alf Alder. The younger kids were tormenting him, so I went round. I had no idea it would turn out like it did. Good job I was there. Dean was close to the edge — another few minutes and who knows?"

"How did he manage to overdose? I'd have thought that crew were pretty adept at drug taking."

"Layla thinks whatever he took was spiked. He had a visitor. Dean didn't have what he'd come to collect. The overdose, I suspect, was his punishment."

"Do we know who the visitor was?" asked Rocco.

"Kane Laycock told me it was 'a mate.'" He shook his head. "I missed him by no more than an hour. Kane's coming in later to give a statement and a description." Calladine looked across the room at Alice. "Would you arrange for Kane to come in late morning. The details of the PC watching his gran's house are with the desk sergeant. And we'll need a child protection officer too. He's unlikely to have a parent with him and he's a vulnerable boy."

"What had this mate come to collect?" asked Ruth. "Money? More drugs? Was Kane able to tell you?"

"No. We'll go and have a word with Dean shortly. If we can get him to talk, so much the better."

"No joy on Tyler Dodd," Rocco said. "The Manchester force reckon he's gone to ground, but they did email over a photo and profile."

"Good, we'll see if young Kane recognises him." He put Dean's mobile in his desk drawer. "Right then, let's see what Julian's got for us."

"Shouldn't you hand that over, sir?" Rocco asked.

"I'd like a quick look first, and no doubt it'll turn out to be more of the same. Numbers we already have with no names."

* * *

"Are we doing anything about Annie and Billy?" Ruth asked as she and Calladine made their way to the Duggan.

"We have to find them first, and that could prove difficult."

"I think Billy Alder is involved in this right up to his neck," Ruth said. "That's why his dad is getting grief from those kids. Billy is at one end of the drug supply and they're at the other."

"How? What part does he play?"

"The kids deliver to the users, they're runners. They get paid a tenner a time and there's no shortage of volunteers. Then there are those like Street, who collect the drugs in bulk, divide and pass onto the runners. This entire thing is a hierarchy. Above Street, I reckon there's Billy. And you have to remember, this entire operation is replicated across the country. Borne out by Sean Barber's notebook."

"Has Billy got the brains?" Calladine asked. "Mind you, he does have the wherewithal, and that's what counts."

"What d'you mean?"

"Think about what he does for a living, Ruth, where he works. He's the transport manager. He's in charge of all those lorries and they go all over Europe. I could kick myself for not realising it before."

"You think the drugs are being brought in by Alder's lorries? If that's so, how come Richard Alder doesn't know?"

"We don't know that he doesn't. This entire thing is huge, Ruth. And Billy isn't the one at the top of the tree, well, not this part of the tree anyway. Like you pointed out, that has to be someone with brains."

"What's your theory?"

"I've no idea. We've interviewed everyone connected with the case. Alder, Pennington, and Billy. I want Billy Alder finding, and interviewed. He ran for a reason, and I'm beginning to think that had little to do with Annie's marriage."

Ruth looked at him. "Any ideas?"

"I want you to speak to Annie's friend, Joanne. Annie will have contacted her about Frankie's funeral. See if you can get her onside. If you must, play the 'Annie might be in danger' card." He smiled grimly. "For all we know, she might be."

"Meanwhile, what will you be up to?"

"Once we've seen Julian, I'm after the evidence I need to get a warrant to search Alder's lorries and stock. I'm also hoping that Dean Laycock has learned his lesson and will talk to me."

* * *

Julian Batho wasn't in his lab for once. "He's gone off somewhere," Natasha Barrington told the pair. "He got a call and was gone within seconds."

Calladine was concerned. In Julian's well-ordered life there was very little, if anything, that would provoke that reaction. "Did he give any hint what it was about?"

"No, and I didn't ask. But before he left, he thrust these results into my hand. Said you'd call in for them."

Natasha's expert eyes scanned the paperwork.

"Seems your lad took an overdose. A dangerous mix of heroin and fentanyl. He's a lucky boy. If you hadn't found him when you did, he might have died."

"My guess is that he didn't take it by choice," Calladine replied as he took the papers from her. "Is Julian on his mobile?"

The pathologist nodded. "I should think so."

Back in the car park, Calladine phoned him. He wanted to make sure whatever had taken Julian away had nothing to do with Zoe and the baby.

"I forgot to pick Aunt Amy up from Oldston station," Julian explained. He sounded a little out of breath. "I left the poor woman standing there with all her luggage for over half an hour."

Instant relief. "Couldn't she have got a taxi?" Calladine said.

"Yes, but she wouldn't be able to get into my flat. Have you picked up the results?"

"Yes, from Natasha. Thanks for that." He rang off and turned to Ruth. "Dean Laycock was given that concoction deliberately. Someone wants him dead."

"Outlived his usefulness?" she suggested. "Got a loose tongue?"

"I don't know, but I intend to find out."

* * *

Calladine dropped Ruth back off at the station and then drove straight to the hospital. A uniformed PC was sitting outside keeping a watchful eye.

"Any visitors?" the inspector asked.

The PC shook his head.

Inside the room Dean Laycock was sitting up in bed. His face was a sickly shade of yellow.

"You've really upset someone this time, Dean," Calladine said to the lad. "Left you for dead, he did. If Alf Alder hadn't rung me, you'd be in the morgue today, not in this bed."

Dean turned his head away. "I'm not up to being questioned. Do one, copper."

"Okay, have it your way, Dean. But the minute we leave you, he'll be back, and this time he might use a knife, like he did with Sean and Frankie."

"Scare tactics. I know what your lot are like."

Calladine was fast losing patience. He leaned in close. "Had I not turned up last night, you'd be dead," he hissed. "Think on that when you're left alone." Calladine made for the door. He was wasting his time.

"Copper!" Dean shouted after him. "Okay, but you'll have to put me somewhere safe, our Kane and me mam too."

CHAPTER 38

Back at the station, Kane Laycock was waiting with the child protection officer, Sarah Grange.

"Go easy, he's nervous," she told Calladine quietly. "He's concerned that he'll drop his brother in it."

Calladine looked at the lad. He was reasonably tidy for once. "It's alright, Kane, just do your best. I've been to see Dean and he's doing well. He's agreed to talk to me too. We will arrange for you, Dean and your mum, if she wants it, to be protected until this is over."

Kane gave Calladine a tentative smile.

Calladine led the way to the soft interview room. "Do you want something to drink?" he offered, but the lad shook his head. Nerves, Calladine decided.

"I'm interested in the people who visited your Dean at the flat. Do you know any of their names?"

The boy nodded. "Some. The main one was that one last night. Dean was scared of him."

"Did he visit often?"

"A few times a week. He kept on at Dean, telling him he wasn't shifting the stuff quick enough. Dean got annoyed but he wasn't having any. He threatened Dean all the time."

"I'm going to show you some photos," Calladine said. "Have a good look and if you see anyone you recognise, tell me."

He handed Kane a photo of Sean Barber.

"That's Barber, he was Dean's mate."

"Did he drive Dean around in that car of his?"

"Yeah, but then someone torched it."

"Do you know who? Did Dean talk about it?"

"I only know that Barber were gutted. Dean said it was a warning."

Calladine showed the boy a photo of Andrew Harvey.

Kane had relaxed a bit and now smiled in recognition. "Andrew, he's alright when he's not off his head. He's always with our Dean."

"Do you know what they got up to?"

"Selling drugs. They paid us lot to take stuff to houses."

"Did you know what Dean was doing?"

"I guessed. Dean was a user and had some dodgy friends, it wasn't hard."

Finally, Calladine showed Kane the photo of Tyler Dodd. "Did this young man ever come to your flat?"

Kane looked up wide eyed. "That's him, the one from last night." He shuddered. "He's creepy. I never saw him smile."

Now they were getting somewhere. "Do you know where he is now?"

Kane shrugged. "He just appears, drops the stuff off, sorts the gangs. You know, tells 'em where to set up next, and then he's gone."

Calladine would have to get on to the Manchester force. Dodd needed finding and quick. He smiled at the lad. "Thanks, Kane, you've been a great help." Too true he had. Now they were finally getting closer to finding the elusive 'Street.'

* * *

Ruth arranged to meet Joanne at her home. She lived in the village of Lowermill, in a flat above the newsagents on the High Street.

"No children round your heels today?" Ruth greeted her. "Bet you welcome time to yourself."

"What d'you want?" came Joanne's sullen reply. She checked her watch. "I have to pick Jack up and bring him here for his lunch soon."

Small talk not welcome, thought Ruth. Fine, she would get straight to the point. "Have you heard from Annie?"

"Why?"

"A simple yes or no will do, Joanne. Annie told me she would contact you about Frankie's funeral. She can't leave it much longer, so she must have phoned you."

"Yes, she did. But before you ask, she wouldn't tell me where they were. She insisted I was better off not knowing."

"But she is coming back? Annie will want to go to her own sister's funeral, surely."

"She didn't say and I didn't ask," Joanne said.

"You do know that the abduction thing was a ruse? Annie took Sophie and tried to extort one million pounds from her husband. Then she ran off with Billy Alder. Were you aware of any of this?"

Joanne's eyes slid away. "Look, you have no idea what she went through. Life with Rick was no picnic. Annie was terrified of him and his new mate, Pennington."

"Yes, she told us. But we can find no evidence for that. Richard appears to be a good bloke and even now wants her back, regardless of what she's done."

"He used to hit her! For God's sake, didn't you see the bruise on her cheek! One word out of turn was enough. Rick has no patience. Annie was afraid that one of these days even Sophie would fall foul of his temper."

"Did you experience his moods first-hand?"

"Well, no. But Annie told me about them often enough. She wouldn't lie to me, she had no reason to. To be honest, I'm glad she found safety with Billy. She has Sophie and they can start again."

"Has she called you? It's a simple matter to get your phone records and check through them."

Joanne folded her arms and walked towards the door. "I've had enough. I want you to go now."

Ruth regarded the woman for a moment or two. "We think there are others looking for Billy, and they won't be so understanding. If we're right, he's made some dangerous enemies. Let's hope we find them before they do."

"If she comes back, I'll speak to her," Joanne muttered. "I'm sure Annie and Billy simply wanted a few days away to clear their heads. Annie has done nothing wrong."

* * *

"Kane Laycock recognised the photo of Tyler Dodd," Calladine told Ruth as she entered the incident room. "Dean has been a bit more forthcoming too."

"Haven't found Street though — now that would be useful. He must had gone to ground. Perhaps running from us, and those at the top. Street is part of this but I doubt he's the main man. He distributes, keeps the gangs under control. It's the guilty party at the top we need."

She saw Calladine frown as he studied the incident board intently. Scrutinising the photos, the notes, and all the lines linking fact to fact.

"Who do we have in the frame?" he asked. "I'm stumped. Richard Alder? Giles Pennington? Perhaps Billy Alder himself? He's in a position to deal with drugs brought into the country in Alder's lorries."

Ruth joined him at the board and tapped one of the latest notes he'd made. "Billy disappears and suddenly there's a shortage. You could be right."

The two detectives shared a look. Ruth spoke. "We should get a warrant, go and take a look."

"I'll speak to Birch," Calladine said, "get it organised." He turned to Rocco. "In the meantime speak to Julian again. Make sure there's no forensic evidence we're unaware of."

CHAPTER 39

"DCI Birch has agreed to organise the warrant," Calladine announced to the team. "She was reluctant, but on the basis that we suspect Billy Alder of being heavily involved in the importation of drugs, she doesn't have much choice."

"I don't expect it'll please Chesworth, either," Ruth whispered.

"We'll leave Chesworth for another day. For now, we'll go and have a word with Richard Alder. I know the warrant isn't in place but we can have a word anyway." He turned to Ruth. "How's your hand?"

"Almost healed."

"You can drive then." He tossed her the car keys. "Did Joanne tell you anything useful?"

"No. She maintains Richard Alder is a bully, and him and Pennington are a force to be reckoned with."

"What do you think?"

Ruth shrugged. "She could be right. Pennington has the right MO and Alder does owe him."

Calladine still wasn't convinced. Pennington might be dodgy. But his gut told him Alder was okay. "How do we play this?"

"By the letter. Once the warrant is in place, we get uniform and the sniffer dogs in. They go over each lorry in turn."

"Those lorries come through customs, and nothing has ever been found." The inspector shook his head. "So what chance do a handful of uniforms and a couple of dogs have?"

Calladine was quiet for most of the drive. They desperately needed a break, but where that would come from, he had no idea.

* * *

Richard Alder was not happy. "We don't do illegal," he insisted. "Our lorries travel across Europe and we have never had any bother." He was staring out of his office windows at the yard below. "Take a look. We've had three in this morning from the continent. Do you want to start with them? Although what you expect to find is a mystery to me."

"We are arranging a warrant, Mr Alder," Calladine said.

"No need, I won't stand in your way. Feel free to go through my premises with a fine-tooth comb. You won't find anything."

He was confident, Calladine gave him that. "If you're sure." He turned and nodded at Ruth. She left the room. "My colleague will muster the troops."

"And Annie? What about her?"

"Your wife and brother are still missing. But, given that she has Frankie's funeral to arrange, I expect she'll be back soon."

Alder sighed. "I hope you're right."

Calladine left him to it and went to find Ruth. She'd gone out into the yard and was looking at the three lorries that were waiting to be unloaded.

Ruth pointed to an area of land by the warehouse. "The containers are taken off the flatbeds across there. The warehouse staff unload and store the goods inside."

"These containers, they don't look anything special."

"We'll look for false walls and all the rest, don't fret. The goods are transported in boxes, we'll get the dogs to sniff around them."

"What's that building there?"

"That's Billy's workshop. A huge chasm of a place, but then it'd have to be to get a flatbed in it."

"Hello!" A man with a clipboard approached them. "Sam Boardman, I work here. I see to the stock when it arrives, tick stuff off, ensure we've got what we ordered."

Calladine introduced himself and Ruth. "This lot here," he pointed at the three lorries. "Which port have they come from?"

"Dover, and then they've travelled overnight," the man said.

"And they get through customs no bother?"

Boardman nodded. "Occasionally one or other of them will be stopped and the contents of the container inspected."

"Is anything ever found?" Ruth asked.

"If you're talking contraband, no." He smiled. "Mr Alder would have their jobs. We've never had any trouble on that score."

"Do you know the last time one of your lorries was gone over by customs?"

"We keep a log. But it's not often. The customs at Dover are so busy they usually work on tip-offs. We have a good reputation, so no bother."

"Your transport manager, Billy Alder, how are things going with him being away?" Calladine asked.

Boardman raised an eyebrow. "Billy's position here is just a title. He isn't required to do very much, so we're not missing him at all. Our priority is to keep the fleet moving. To that end, we have adequate warehouse staff and a workshop full of mechanics."

Calladine heard his mobile beep. "The warrant is in place," he smiled at Ruth. "Mr Boardman, we have a warrant to search these premises. We intend to concentrate on your lorries and the stock that is brought into the country."

"What are you looking for?" Boardman asked with a frown.

"Drugs, sir." The short answer.

Within the hour the search was in full swing. The containers were open and the stock being gone over box by box.

"The workshop is quiet today," Ruth remarked to Boardman, who was fussing around the uniforms.

"It's the weekend skeleton staff," he said, checking his clipboard, "which today means Tyler. He'll be finishing off a job ready for Monday."

"Tyler? Tyler Dodd?" Ruth was suddenly alert. "We'll have to take a look inside." She pushed open the large double doors. The huge room was quiet, and apart from a flatbed lorry parked up, was empty. "No Tyler," she told Boardman.

The man shrugged. "Probably gone for his break. Be careful in there, it's a dangerous place if you don't know what you're doing."

"What's this one in for?" she pointed at the lorry.

Boardman checked his sheet. "It's one that came in this morning. The driver reported that it was running sluggish, so engine problem."

Cutting and welding gear were laid out on the workbench. Ruth was no expert on vehicle repairs but whoever was working on the lorry appeared to be interested in the steel beam that ran the length of the flatbed rather than the engine. She took a closer look. There was a cut in the metal the length of the beam.

"Tom!" she called out. "Get one of the dogs in here."

Calladine appeared at her side. "Found something?"

"There's work being done on this. Engine, allegedly, but the mechanic's nowhere to be found and look at this." She pointed at the tools on the workbench.

"Cutting gear. Why, I wonder?" He ran his hand over the surface of the beam.

"It's round here!" Ruth shouted. "A piece of the steel has been cut. It looks as if someone wants to remove a piece from this side."

"Mr Boardman," Calladine called. "Do you have someone who can finish this?"

Sam Boardman peered closely at the beam and frowned. "This work isn't on the job sheet. What's Tyler playing at?"

Calladine studied the beam. "This has been cut and re-welded a number of times. You can see where the previous welds have been."

"I'll get a welder to take a look."

"Very clever!" Ruth said once Boardman had left. "I reckon there's one or more cavities in this beam and that's where the drugs are stashed." Calladine went for a word with one of the dog handlers, and then turned his attention to Boardman. "This Tyler, do you have a description?"

"I can do better than that, I've got his employment record in the office."

"With a photo?"

"Of course."

CHAPTER 40

"Tyler Dodd has been working at Alder's." Calladine had assembled the team when he and Ruth got back to the station. "He worked on the lorries. A good welder, according to his boss."

Rocco was looking at the photos that had been taken of the lorry and the supporting beam. "So they hide the drugs inside. They could have been at this for ages. Dodd retrieves and distributes the drugs."

Alice spoke. "What about Billy? He was transport manager, he can't have been oblivious."

Calladine nodded in agreement. "We still can't find him. But given that he's not returned, we have to assume that he is involved."

"Is Billy at the top of this tree?" Alice asked.

"I'm still not sure." Calladine frowned. "Billy likes the easy life, a night out, getting away with doing as little as possible. I just don't see him as a top-notch crook."

"Richard Alder has to be implicated. It's his firm," Ruth pointed out.

"I'm not sure about him either, Ruth."

"We can't keep ruling people out!" she glared at him.

"What we need is to bring in Tyler Dodd, and quickly. The Manchester force couldn't find him because he was hiding under our very noses!"

The office phone rang and Alice answered it. "Sir," she called. "Billy Alder has been found."

"Are they bringing him in?"

She shook her head. "No, sir. He's dead. They found him in his car this morning, head bashed in."

There was a stunned silence. Calladine thought hard. Was this the top man's revenge because Billy ran out on him? Or a rival gang's attempt at a takeover? Whatever it was, it complicated matters even further. "We'd better go and take a look. Where was he found?"

"The waste ground by the Hobfield."

"Same as Frankie. Any sign of Annie?"

"There was no mention," Alice confirmed.

Calladine looked at Ruth. "Go and have another word with Joanne. Tell her about Billy. If she does know where Annie is, she might tell you now."

Calladine sat down at his desk. With Billy out of the frame, that left Richard Alder and Giles Pennington. With his past, Pennington was favourite. He'd bring him in again. Present the man with the new evidence and see what he had to say.

"Rocco, bring Pennington in for another chat. I'll go and have a look at the crime scene before they take Billy to the Duggan."

* * *

Police tape had been stretched around a large area, where the CSI team in their white disposable overalls were hard at work. "It's to keep them little urchins out," a uniform explained, pointing at the tape. "But to be fair, they're upset. Billy coached the footy team and they knew him."

"Billy's dad, Alf, does he know?" Calladine asked.

210

"A PC's gone up there now. His brother Richard's been told, too."

That was good, no need for him to go round just yet. "Let's have a look."

"He's in the driver's seat, sir. Whoever did this swiped him with something heavy from behind."

"What sort of heavy?"

"Metal, I'd say," Natasha said, joining them. "Faint traces of rust in the wound. But, as always, I'll know more after the PM and we've run tests."

"Murder then?"

"Well, he didn't do that to himself, Tom."

"How long's he been dead?"

"No more than twelve hours. Can we move the body out now?"

Calladine walked towards the car. Billy was slumped over the steering wheel, a bloody wound on the back of his skull. "Okay. Let me know when you do the PM. We are desperate for a break in this case — any forensics, get them to me fast," he instructed. "Have you found any further forensics with either the Barber or Halliwell murders?"

Natasha shook her head. "I'm afraid not. Sean Barber had been set upon by a mob, that made things tricky. Frankie Halliwell was found in the open. It was muddy and had been raining, so not much luck there either."

Calladine's mobile rang. It was Ruth. She sounded excited. "I've finally found Annie. She's with Sophie at Joanne's place. I've asked her to come in but she's refusing. Says she's done nothing wrong and wants to be left alone."

"Did she say anything about Billy?"

"Only that she'd left him."

"Where are you now?"

"I'm in my car outside Joanne's flat keeping an eye. She might try to run again."

"Does she know Billy's dead?"

"I didn't tell her, but she doesn't seem upset about anything."

"I'll send a uniform to replace you. I need you back at the station."

* * *

"We now know Annie's whereabouts," Calladine told the team. "We'll speak to her shortly and break the news about Billy. He's been murdered within the last twelve hours. Ideas anyone?"

Ruth spoke. "The obvious candidate is Tyler Dodd. He wasn't at Alder's workshop when we visited earlier, and we now know what he was up to. It's likely that Billy did too."

"Billy runs because he knows the score, has possibly been threatened. If he doesn't go along with what Tyler wants, he's a dead man," Rocco said.

Calladine nodded. It sounded plausible.

"We're still short of someone at the top. Billy's murder means it wasn't him. That leaves Alder and Pennington."

"Would Richard Alder kill his own brother?" Alice asked.

Rocco's eyes were fixed on the boss's desk. "Can anyone else hear that phone? It's faint, but I think it's coming from your desk, sir."

Calladine suddenly remembered the phone he'd taken from Dean Laycock's flat when he'd taken the overdose. He'd intended to get it looked at, but had forgotten.

He retrieved the mobile from the drawer and looked at the caller. On the screen was one word — 'Street.' He picked up the office phone and dialled the techies. "I want to know which mast a caller pinged a few moments ago." He gave them the number on Dean's screen. "This is urgent," he told them.

"Dodd?" Ruth asked once he'd hung up.

"I don't think so." He showed her the display.

The techies were on it and got back quickly. "The location of the mobile with that number is Lowermill High Street," they told Calladine.

That was unexpected. Had he been wrong, and it was in fact Alder masterminding the drug dealing, and he'd found out where Annie was? It was risky, but he had to know. Calladine rang the number back. The seconds ticked by. He waited. A female voice answered. "I've got work for you," she said. There was no mistaking the voice. It was Annie. In a flash he realised how utterly they'd been duped. He was angry — with her for what she'd done, but most of all with himself for not even suspecting her.

The team were waiting expectantly. "Well?" asked Ruth.

"Lowermill High Street," he said slowly. "That means . . ."

"Annie Alder." Ruth finished the sentence for him. "I'll tell the PC on watch to bring her in."

"She's dangerous, he'll need help. Make sure he has it."

Calladine sat down at his desk. Annie Alder. The drugs, the killings, was all that down to her? Or did she have an accomplice? And why had no one she had dealt with ever mention that she was a woman? He groaned inwardly. Because she always texted them, that was why.

CHAPTER 41

Annie Alder sat quietly in the interview room. Calladine stood in the adjoining room watching her through the one-way window. He couldn't work out what had motivated her to carry out those crimes. The drug dealing was obviously for money, which didn't make sense because her husband was a wealthy man. What bothered Calladine were the murders. Was she responsible for any, or all, of those? He turned on his heel and went back to the incident room.

"Right. Ruth you're with me," he said. "This isn't going to be pleasant, and I'd value your help. Annie has lied and pulled the wool over our eyes consistently throughout this case. You have spoken to her more than the rest of us, she might open up to you. We need the truth, and quick. This case has dragged on for long enough." He saw Ruth check the office clock. "I know it's late, are you okay with this?"

Ruth nodded. "I want the truth every bit as much as you do. Let's get on with it."

"Annie, you should have a solicitor to advise you," Ruth said as the two detectives entered the interview room. "We can get one for you."

"No need, I've done nothing wrong."

She was confident. Gone was the scared, tearful woman they had become accustomed to.

"Why did you ring that mobile number earlier?" Calladine began.

"I got the wrong number, my mistake." She smiled.

"You spoke to me. What did you mean by 'I've got work for you?'"

"I thought you were someone else, the gardener I use."

"Rubbish! You thought you were talking to Dean Laycock."

Annie looked from one detective to the other. "I've no idea what you're talking about."

Dean Laycock's name had made her nervous. She was pulling at the sleeve of the jumper she wore, tugging it over the palm of her right hand.

"Have you hurt yourself, Annie?" Ruth asked her.

"I'm fine."

"Do you know that Billy's dead, murdered?" Ruth asked.

"No, I didn't. But me and Billy are over. I haven't seen him in days."

There was no hint of emotion on her face. She didn't care. A man she'd left her husband for, a man she was prepared to start a new life with, had been killed, and all she could do was shrug it off.

"You don't give a damn about Billy, do you?" Calladine said.

"You wouldn't understand."

"Try me."

"I don't want to go over it again, it's too raw."

Calladine was fast losing patience. It was late and she would run rings around them all night if it suited.

"We believe you've been smuggling drugs into the country in your husband's lorries."

"You're off your head. You must be if you imagine I could do that!"

"You weren't on your own, Annie. You had Tyler Dodd and Billy to help you. Billy get cold feet, did he?"

215

"I have no idea what you're talking about."

"Annie, tell us the truth," Ruth said gently. "We'll be here all night otherwise and you've got Sophie to think of."

Annie looked at Ruth. A smile played on her lips. "You're right, Ruth. I've got to go, Sophie needs me." She turned her attention to Calladine. "Do you have any evidence against me apart from calling a wrong number?"

Calladine was not about to let her worm her way out of this. He stood up. "We've not finished yet. Keep an eye on her," he told the uniform.

"She's right," Ruth grumbled as they walked down the corridor. "We have nothing concrete. No Dodd, Billy's dead, so no statement from him. Do you think Dean Laycock will identify her?"

"Unlikely, Ruth."

Calladine was annoyed, too. All along he'd known Annie was playing her own game but not once did he think she was their 'Mr Big.'

"It's not going well," he told Rocco and Alice back in the incident room. "We need more than that phone call to throw at her. She might look sweet and innocent, but Annie Alder is far from that, believe me."

"I've rung the Duggan, guv," Rocco said. "CSI have completed their search of Alder's workshops. They found cocaine residue in the cavities in that flatbed. Julian says to give him another hour and he may have something we can use."

Good old Julian, that was if there was anything to find. Calladine sighed wearily.

"Oh, and Bill Geddes is waiting for you downstairs," Rocco added.

"I'll go and see what he wants. He might have something useful, he did give us Andrew Harvey. We'll take a break and try again," he told Ruth.

Geddes was sitting in reception, a large envelope in his hands. "Inspector Calladine, I've got something for you."

Calladine took the envelope from him. "What's this?"

"Something you'll find useful. I picked up a lot of useful skills being with the group. How to blend into the shadows for one. I've been watching you. For days now I've been on your tail," he admitted. "But I drew the line at following you to Wales." He smiled.

This was news to Calladine. He'd had no idea he'd been followed.

"I've also spoken to people you interviewed. Most were cagey, but Alf Alder was happy to talk. The night the ambulance carted off that lad, I hung around outside."

"I left a uniformed officer watching that flat, he never reported seeing you."

Geddes laughed at the surprised look on Calladine's face. "He wouldn't, like I said, I'm good at not being seen. I've had a lot of practice recently."

"I thought you'd done with all that."

"I have. I've ditched the vigilantes. I haven't the stomach for it, as I said. But I still need justice for my boy. I couldn't just let it drop. He was part of something much bigger than simple bullying. I worked that much out."

"You were taking a risk."

"It's my neck on the line," he said. "Anyway, I was round the back of the car park. I waited for an hour or more and then decided to go home. I walked over the waste ground back to the town."

"You saw who killed Billy Alder," Calladine said.

"I certainly did, and it came as a shock I'll tell you. I would have intervened, but it was too late, the bloke was already dead."

Calladine opened the envelope and pulled out a sheaf of photographs. There were at least ten. One caught his eye. Annie Alder closing the driver's door. She was dressed in dark clothing and wearing a hoodie, but there was no doubt it was her. She was turned face-on towards the camera.

"What she did sickened me, I couldn't let it go. I followed her. I didn't know what I was going to do. I toyed with the idea of tackling her, but thought better of it. That's one dangerous lady. Halfway along Leesdon High Street, she threw this in a bin." He held up a bloodied wrench in a plastic bag. "It was far enough away from the crime scene, I bet she thought it'd never be found."

* * *

Calladine sent the wrench straight to Julian at the Duggan. He wanted proof that it had Billy Alder's blood on it, and, with luck, there might be fingerprints.

"We've got her," he announced to the team. "Bill Geddes saw Annie kill Billy. He's been following us, was anyone aware of that?"

They shook their heads. "It doesn't surprise me," Ruth admitted. "Losing his son like that cut him to shreds. He's had no closure, no one has been prosecuted. This is his way."

"We have photos too. I intend to charge Annie Alder with Billy's murder and lock her up overnight. Tomorrow we'll have the results off Julian. Let's see her wriggle out of this one."

Calladine packed up for the night on a high. Annie had screamed the place down when he'd charged her. Flew at him in a rage, shrieking that she didn't do it. Calladine had phoned Richard Alder and told him to pick up his daughter. He'd been shocked, admitted that never in a million years would he have suspected her. But he was thrilled to have Sophie home and safe.

"Calladine, congratulations." It was DCI Birch. "You've got your breakthrough, I believe."

"Yes ma'am. A member of the public came forward with vital evidence."

"An update for you. It will be common knowledge soon enough but for now, keep it to yourself. Isaac Chesworth has resigned. It won't stop the investigation — he was receiving regular payments from an account in the name of Wendy Jones."

"An alias of Annie Alder's. She was paying him to turn a blind eye."

"And to ensure that if there were any hiccups at the ports, they were rectified swiftly."

"Does that mean you're staying with us, ma'am?"

"No, I'm still leaving in a couple of months. I suggest you get your application in for DCI."

CHAPTER 42

Day 10

"Julian must have been working through the night," Calladine told the team. "We owe him. Annie Alder's prints were on that wrench and they found traces of both hers and Billy Alder's blood."

Ruth looked confused. "How did Annie's blood get on it?"

"Julian reckons she'll have a scrape on the palm of her right hand. The wrench was rusty, rough to the touch. She must have gripped it so tight that it grazed her hand."

"She was fussing with her hand yesterday," Ruth recalled. "I bet she didn't want us to see."

"Do we check that?" Alice asked.

"Yes. We'll interview her again shortly." He paused, looking round at his team. "We've got her on Billy's murder, but that's it. We have no evidence that Annie was responsible for the deaths of Sean Barber or Frankie Halliwell, or that she smuggled and distributed the drugs."

"So how do we get that evidence?" Ruth asked.

"We need Tyler Dodd. Alert the local forces, I want him found."

* * *

Annie Alder had a solicitor at her side for the next interview.

"We have some new evidence, Annie," Calladine began. He laid out a couple of the photos Bill Geddes had given him. "Tell me what you see."

"A woman getting out of a car."

"That's you, Annie," he pointed. "We can all see your face quite clearly. What is it you have in your right hand?"

She was fiddling with the sleeve of her jumper again.

"Hurt yourself, Annie?" Ruth asked. "Let me see, it might need attention."

"Leave me alone!" Annie spat. "I've done nothing wrong!"

"You've grazed your hand, haven't you? That wrench you hit Billy with was old and rusty. You gripped it tight and it cut your palm."

Her expression was thunderous. "Rubbish! You're off your head."

"The wrench has Billy's blood on it." Calladine paused, letting this sink in. "Yours too."

Annie looked at the two detectives with wild eyes.

"We have all the evidence we need to charge you with murder," Calladine told her.

She nodded at the photos. "Who took those?"

"Never mind that now, just tell us what happened."

Think you're clever, don't you? But you're not. You're stupid, the lot of you. Me and Billy have run rings around you lot for weeks and you didn't have a clue."

Calladine decided to take advantage. "Tell us, Annie, put us straight. You're right, we had no idea. All this time, we've been after someone else."

"You've been chasing shadows, I had you all fooled," she said proudly. "I organised the drugs coming in. I found the contacts, had Billy fix the lorries fixed so nothing could be found."

"Where did you get the idea?"

"Pennington." She smirked. "Not that he helped me. He's really an ex-con from Glasgow, did you know that?"

"We know all about Pennington," Calladine said. "But it's you we're interested in."

"I tried to frame him by getting both Barber and Laycock to phone him. I knew you'd check his phone records. Given his past, you had to suspect him. If you'd dug further, you'd have found out that I used the same method he did. Billy found out about his antics from years ago and I decided to have a go myself. Doctoring the flatbeds was something Pennington did back in his Glasgow days."

"Why fake Sophie's disappearance and make the ransom demand?"

"I faked the kidnap to get my share of the money from Rick. I wanted a divorce and I wanted him ruined. I reckoned that a million out of the assets would set him back so far that the firm would never recover. I helped to make that factory a success, I deserved every penny of that money." She leaned forward. "If you hadn't interfered, he'd have paid up. I suppose you'll tell him. Well, I'm glad. I want him to know it was me. To know that I'm cleverer than he ever was. He'll hate that."

"Weren't you making enough money from selling drugs?"

"It's a lucrative scam but it won't last. Sooner or later the big boys will move in and take over."

"And Billy, what did he do to deserve his fate?"

"Billy got scared. He knew Rick suspected we were having an affair."

"And were you? Having an affair?" Calladine asked.

"God no! Billy was a means to an end. He did as he was told."

"What about Isaac Chesworth? What hold do you have over him?" Calladine asked.

"He's a womaniser," she smirked. "He likes them young too. In fact, the younger the better. He came on to Frankie the night of her birthday party at the Country Club. She was no angel and led him on." She gave a shrug. "She wheedled a lot of information out of him about other girls he'd been with. We set him up with an underage friend of Frankie's and the rest was a doddle. I have photos of them together if you want to see. Doing as I told him was preferable to losing his job and his pension."

The woman was ruthless. She'd do anything to get what she wanted.

"You acted the part of the frantic mother well," Ruth said. "You took us all in."

"While you were feeling sorry for me and searching for Sophie, you weren't seeing what was really going on. Cheap drugs and plenty of it. The punters are happy and we made a fortune."

"Did you kill Frankie?" Short and to the point. Annie stared at Calladine.

A look of indignation crossed her face. "Of course not, she was my sister. Billy did that. He stabbed her. Didn't you find the knife?" she asked slyly.

"Yes, where it was left for us, wrapped in a plastic bag with Pennington's prints on it and taped to the underside of a car he'd used."

"Frankie became a pain. Always whining about Billy and him being with me. She was going to tell Rick about us." She paused. "She would have, too. Not that me and Billy were serious or anything. Billy was terrified of Rick. I didn't want Frankie to die, but Billy wouldn't listen to reason."

"How did he kill her?" Calladine asked.

"With the knife, both her and that kid who outed me. Clever little bugger, he was."

"Which kid?" Calladine asked.

"Sean Barber. He got greedy. Asked me for money to keep quiet. Billy got scared, so he sorted it. I thought those hooligans who beat him up would get the blame. Pity."

"We only have your word for that, Annie. Billy can no longer speak for himself."

She smirked at Calladine. "I'm not stupid, Inspector. I kept the clothes he was wearing both times. Check them, you'll find Frankie's blood on one set and Barber's on the other."

"How did you contact the others who worked for you?" Ruth asked.

She smiled. "I texted them. Well I couldn't let them hear my voice, could I? They might have guessed."

"So, you are Street." Calladine nodded. "That clears that one up."

* * *

Both Calladine and Ruth were exhausted. Annie had confessed, they had their answers, so it was over. What questions were left could wait for tomorrow.

Back in the incident room Rocco, Alice, and even Thorpe clapped as they entered.

"Well done, both," Alice smiled. "You got her."

"Tyler Dodd has been picked up by the Stockport police. He was on the motorway when they stopped him for speeding, the idiot!" Rocco said

That rounded the case off nicely, now they had them all. Calladine should have felt elated, planning a few pints in the Wheatsheaf, but the case had drained him.

"I'm whacked," Calladine told the team. "Despite only being lunchtime, I'll think I'll call it a day. See you all in the morning."

EPILOGUE

Day 11

"Birch is leaving?" Ruth looked shocked. "I didn't see that coming."

It was just the pair of them in the incident room the following morning, so Calladine saw no harm in telling her. "She told me a few days ago," he admitted. "And she wants me to go for DCI."

"Acting?"

"Initially, but I will apply to make it permanent. She reckons I have a good chance."

Ruth looked doubtful.

"Come on, out with it."

"I don't know what I think about that bit of news," she huffed. "You'll change. You won't be the same. The dynamic of the team will shift."

"I doubt that, Ruth. I'm too long in the tooth to make big changes with the job. I have a decision to make. It's either jump in at the deep end and go for it, or . . ."

Ruth looked at him, hands on hips. Dare he tell her?

"Or what?" she demanded.

"Retirement."

The word hung in the air as the pair stared at each other. Calladine could only guess at what she was thinking.

"Promotion it is then," Ruth finally said. "All other alternatives are off the menu. But if power goes to your head, Calladine, you'll get the sharp end of my tongue."

That was him told. But the retirement option couldn't be forgotten easily. He'd thought about it a lot recently.

"What are we doing about Annie?" Ruth changed the subject.

"She will make a statement and then we'll pass the case on to the CPS."

"She surprised me, you know. Annie fooled us all."

"Are you alright to hold the fort?" He checked the time. "I promised to pop round for a coffee with Zoe and the others. Talk baby stuff. I should make an effort, Amy's come a long way."

"Go on then, get off," she urged. "And don't let Amy browbeat you into anything."

* * *

Ruth knew him only too well. Calladine was nervous about seeing Amy again. It'd been her who'd broke it off when she'd moved to Cornwall. Calladine had been disappointed. He liked the woman and had hoped they would have a future together.

"You sorted the case I hear," Zoe said, kissing his cheek. "Takes off some of the stress.".

"Certainly does. It's damned hard when you work for days on end and get nowhere."

She took his hand and led him through. "We're in the back. Amy's talked about little else but seeing you again."

Should he be flattered? He had butterflies in his stomach. It was a long time since that had happened with any woman, even Layla. He spotted Amy at once. She looked much as he remembered her, with long, flowing hair, and gypsy-style skirt. She was wearing a matching top with several sets of beads around her neck. She walked towards him, a smile on her face.

"Amy, you're looking good," he said.

"Tom." She gave him a beaming smile, her arms outstretched. "You not being in my life is what's wrong with Cornwall," she admitted. "I've missed you so much."

She took him in her arms and kissed his cheek. "Are you well? You look a little tired."

"I'm fine," he said.

"I hear you've been working hard, not much time for a break."

He shrugged. "The nature of the job, I'm afraid."

She was staring at him, her eyes half closed. He knew that look. Amy considered herself a psychic. She reckoned she was able to see into the future, sense things. Not that Calladine ever took that aspect of her world too seriously. But others did. When she'd owned the new age shop in Leesdon, she was never without customers.

"The time I've spent away from you has made me realise a great truth, Tom," she whispered. "We should be together. I think you know that too."

"Cornwall is some distance, and there's my job . . ."

"Which you are thinking of ditching. It's in your head, spinning round and round. I can feel it." She ran a long finger down his face. "Take care of yourself, Tom. You will get that promotion, but be warned, it might not suit you. Change your mind and you know where I am."

Calladine had no idea how she could possibly know about the promotion. So far, he'd only told Ruth. But Amy was a shrewd woman. When they were together, he'd made no secret of how demanding his job was. It was also reasonable to assume that eventually, even he would be offered promotion. "That is hush-hush for the time being," he whispered back.

Amy gave him one of her enigmatic smiles. "I know something else you will find interesting. The baby is a girl. You are going to have a granddaughter!"

THE END

ALSO BY HELEN H. DURRANT

THE DCI GRECO BOOKS
Book 1: DARK MURDER
Book 2: DARK HOUSES
Book 3: DARK TRADE
Book 4: DARK ANGEL

THE CALLADINE & BAYLISS MYSTERY SERIES
Book 1: DEAD WRONG
Book 2: DEAD SILENT
Book 3: DEAD LIST
Book 4: DEAD LOST
Book 5: DEAD & BURIED
Book 6: DEAD NASTY
Book 7: DEAD JEALOUS
Book 8: DEAD BAD
Book 8: DEAD GUILTY

MATT BRINDLE
Book 1: HIS THIRD VICTIM
Book 2: THE OTHER VICTIM

RACHEL KING
NEXT VICTIM

Join our mailing list now to get bargain book offers from your favourite authors and news on the next Helen H. Durrant mystery:

http://www.joffebooks.com/contact/

FREE KINDLE BOOKS

Please join our mailing list for free kindle crime thriller, detective, mystery, and romance books and new releases, as well as news on the next mystery!
http://www.joffebooks.com/contact/

DO YOU LOVE FREE AND BARGAIN BOOKS?

Thank you for reading this book. If you enjoyed it please leave feedback on Amazon, and if there is anything we missed or you have a question about then please get in touch. The author and publishing team appreciate your feedback and time reading this book.

Our email is office@joffebooks.com

http://joffebooks.com

Follow us on facebook www.facebook.com/joffebooks for news on Helen Durrant's next book

We hate typos but sometimes they slip through. Please send any errors you find to corrections@joffebooks.com We'll get them fixed ASAP. We're very grateful to eagle-eyed readers who take the time to contact us.

Made in the USA
San Bernardino, CA
01 June 2019